house without walls

CH
BURMA
Hanoi
LAOS
Rangoon
THAILAND
Bangkok
VIETNAM
ANDAMAN
SEA
CAMBODIA
GULF OF
THAILAND
My Tho
Ho Chi
Minh City
MALAYSIA
Singapore
"Coconut Island"

SOUTHEAST ASIA

NA

house without walls

May 10, 1979 to June 7, 1980

CHING YEUNG RUSSELL

This is a work of fiction. Any references to historical events, real people, or real places are used fictitiously. Other names, characters, places, and events are products of the author's imagination, and any resemblance to actual events or places or persons, living or dead, is entirely coincidental.

251 Park Avenue South, New York, NY 10010

Manufactured in the United States of America LAK 0519
First Edition
1 3 5 7 9 10 8 6 4 2
Library of Congress Cataloging-in-Publication Data is available upon request.
ISBN 978-1-4998-0875-9
yellowjacketreads.com

To Blake and Morgan, my grandchildren,
and to all the refugees in the world

In memory of my cousin, Chi-Yen Chan

PROLOGUE

I met Lam and *Dee Dee* (their fictionalized names), the protagonists in this story, in 1986. I knew they had been boat people from Vietnam. At first, this didn't excite me. Later, when we grew closer, they talked about what had happened to them while they were on their journey. Theirs was a truly hazardous experience, one that most people could not even imagine. That's why I decided to work on their story. I interviewed them both many times, asking them why they wanted to leave their hometown and about the circumstances in their country in 1979, when they tried to escape.

The information that follows may aid you in your understanding as you journey through this book.

The North Vietnamese Communists took over Saigon, the capital of South Vietnam, on April 30, 1975. The new Communist government mostly targeted ethnic Chinese, also called Hoa, Han, or Chinese Vietnamese, and forced them out of the country. Many of these ethnic Chinese lived in the Cholon district of Saigon. They had their own traditional culture, language, and schools, even though their schools were required to offer Vietnamese lessons. Although they made up only about 5.5 percent of the population in South Vietnam (more than half of them were Cantonese, and the Teochew, Hakka, Hokkien, and Hainanese made up the rest), since they were favored by the French when they colonized Vietnam, they controlled up to 70 to 80 percent of the commerce. The new government closed down the privately owned businesses in early 1978. They seized their businesses and properties and sent many businessmen to reeducation camps, which were located in the remote countryside. Many of those who were sent there didn't come back. Some of them died from hard work or snake bites, or they were killed by the land mines. That's why they wanted to escape.

Some young men, like *Daigo,* the older brother in this story, fled the country to avoid being drafted to fight against China at the border between China and Vietnam in 1979, in which tens of thousands of young people died on both sides. Even though the war officially ended in March of 1979, a couple of months before Lam and *Dee Dee* escaped, some feared that the war would erupt again and that they would be conscripted to fight.

Some people who left Vietnam were seeking political asylum. Those who had fought for the South Vietnamese against the Vietcong (North Vietnam Communists) or who had aided the Americans during the war were considered to be enemies of the country and were sent to reeducation camps or prosecuted.

Some people fled their country because they didn't want to live under communist rule and wanted to seek a better life for themselves and their children. That's why more than one million Vietnamese and ethnic Chinese left Vietnam. Most of them fled by boat.

According to my sources, people over sixteen had to

pay eight taels—more than ten ounces—of gold for a seat on a boat to escape. For children under sixteen, the price was six taels. The gold was reportedly shared between the new government and the people who organized the escapes. After giving the government their share, they would use part of the gold to buy a boat and hire a crew to operate it for the voyage. Therefore, these escapes were open. But sometimes these escapes were arranged on the black market, and only the organizers were paid. In that case, the authorities would try to impede these escapes. That's why people were very careful.

Most of the boat people didn't make it. Many of them died at sea from starvation, dehydration, or drowning, or they were killed by pirates. Even if they were lucky and made it to one of the Southeast Asian countries, many were turned back toward the sea. Some said initially Singapore was the first country to prevent the boat people from entering its coastlines because of their limited land. Singapore provided the refugees with water, food, and fuel before turning them away. (Later, however, they couldn't prevent others from landing. Between 1975 and 1979, nearly five thousand refugees came to Singapore, most of whom were picked up by commercial ships.) However, after Singapore first turned away the boat people, other countries soon began to refuse them sanctuary.

Since the coastline of Malaysia is long, many refugees landed there easily when they first spotted land. The Malaysian government let them stay temporarily and waited for other countries to accept them. But the progress was too slow. They could not adequately provide for the great number of refugees who arrived in this burgeoning armada. That's why they had to tow the latecomers, with water and food provided, back to sea, hoping they would land elsewhere.

Refugees were housed in camps in Hong Kong, Thailand, Indonesia, Malaysia, and the Philippines. Some refugees had to stay in these camps for more than ten years. According to published reports, over twenty-one years, more than 840,000 refugees landed in the countries of Southeast Asia. More than 755,000 of these were resettled in the West, and more than 81,000 were eventually repatriated back to Vietnam under an agreement with the United Nations High Commissioner for Refugees.

Neither Lam nor *Dee Dee* knew the places where they settled down temporarily in Malaysia. When they lived in the camps, they witnessed people dying from snake bites, from diarrhea due to unsanitary conditions, or from drowning while fishing on rafts that they made.

In addition to hearing their story, I also visited a refugee camp in Hong Kong in 1992. (There refugees could learn

English or simple skills inside the camp and some even had permission to go outside the camp to work.) Despite the fact that some refugees who had fled Vietnam up to a decade before were still there and were facing being sent back to Vietnam under a plan by the United Nations High Commissioner for Refugees, they told me their stories about how they got out of Vietnam and how horrible their journey was at sea. *House Without Walls* is a story based on Lam and *Dee Dee*'s accounts, other first-person narratives I heard during my visit to the Hong Kong refugee camp, and my own creativity. In writing this story, I have gained tremendous respect for all people throughout the world who risk their lives for freedom and a better life.

In *House Without Walls*, I strove to portray the perilous journey that some of these refugees faced when they fled their homeland. There are many more cruel details of the escapes. Because this book is for young readers, I edited out some of the more shocking details of cruelty I heard about, but I certainly did not shy away from some of the grittier aspects of the refugee experience. I also emphasized that no matter what life throws at them, children are children—they will still find a way to play, to laugh, and to find joy despite gruesome circumstances—despite living in a "house without walls."

PART ONE

May 10, 1979
Cholon, Vietnam

1 | THE LAST MEAL

An hour before dawn,
Ah Mah and my *ma* want us to have a full stomach
before we leave home.
They stayed up all night, fixing my favorite wontons
and *Daigo* and *Dee Dee*'s beloved Singapore fried noodles.

Daigo and *Dee Dee* eat little.
I don't feel like eating, either,
but I toy the food with a spoon.
My favorite wontons are left
uneaten.

I am sad to leave my family.
I am sad to leave my home.
I am uncertain of this dangerous gamble.

We could drown in the ocean,
capsized by the high waves and strong winds.

We could be robbed by pirates,
raped by them,
or sold to other places as prostitutes.

We could die from starvation or dehydration
in the wide-open sea.

Our lives will be in nature's hands.

But I am willing to take those risks.
For I know
Kwun Yum will
bless *Dee Dee,*
Daigo, and
me.

2 | MY *BABA*

I have fear and hatred in my heart
as the plainclothes police
from the new government
come to our house
unexpectedly,
anytime,
day or night,
just to interrogate *Ma* or *Ah Mah*,
to ask where *Baba* is.

Baba escaped arrest two years ago.
We owned a small family-run grocery.
We feared the new government
would eventually send him,
like other business owners,
to a reeducation camp
where he might die from a snake bite
or hard, risky work, like
clearing the jungle, digging wells,
or sweeping land mines without proper equipment.

That's why my *baba* risked his life,
though reluctant to separate from his whole family,
to become one of the boat people of 1976.
Now he is settled in San Francisco, in America.

3 | MY WISH

I wish that
I could follow in *Baba*'s footsteps.
When the police come,
they don't want to leave.
They stall, staying
as long as they please.
We are powerless, just watching
them search our house and
try to take my *ma*'s gold jewelry.

They watch our
every move,
like ghost shadows
we can't get rid of.

They prick up their ears,
eavesdropping on our conversations.
We can't even talk!

I wish that
I could run far,
far away
to be united with *Baba*
where
nobody would keep a hateful eye

on us or follow us;
where
nobody would enter our home
like it was a public building.

4 | *DAIGO* AND *DEE DEE*

Daigo is fifteen.
He has to go away
to avoid being drafted
to fight with China at the border.

Dee Dee is seven.
He will go with *Daigo,*
to make a better life for himself, *Ma* says.

Ah Mah secretly arranged their escape
just as the war erupted
a few months ago.

I envy them
because they are boys.
They will carry on our family name.

Not me.
Not a girl.

5 | SURPRISE

But then, surprisingly, *Ma* and *Ah Mah*
say they want me to go with my brothers.
That way, I can cook for them
and take care of them
until they get married.
Then their wives will cook for them
and take care of them,
like my *ma* does;
like *Ah Mah* does.

I am overjoyed.
As long as I can get away from the police,
I don't mind
even if we might not
be reunited with *Baba,*
as my family is hoping for,
but end up somewhere else in the world.

So *Ma* and *Ah Mah* collect eighteen taels of pure gold
for the three of us to get on a boat.
It is the usual price for a child under sixteen:
six taels for a child,
eight taels for an adult.

6 | READY

Ah Mah looks at the clock on the wall,
afraid that the police will come in.
She hurries us to get ready.

We are not allowed to carry anything by hand.
It would arouse the suspicion of the police
on the street,
and if everybody took their belongings,
it would overload the boat.

Ma helps *Dee Dee* wrap a small bag
around his waist.
It contains saltines,
beef jerky,
pork jerky,
dried banana chips,
a thin towel, a toothbrush,
and a folded plastic sheet.
Ma also helps *Dee Dee* put on three more cotton shirts
and three more pairs of pants with elastic waists.
On top of them, she adds a raincoat
because it is raining.

Dee Dee jokes,
"I can't walk!

I look like a clumsy elephant!"
But no one laughs.
Ma simply instructs, "Be careful not to lose your shirts."
"I won't," *Dee Dee* promises.
Daigo has copied *Baba*'s address in America
on the underside of *Dee Dee*'s shirt.

While *Daigo* wraps up his own food and dresses himself,
Ma helps me tie my bag.
When she lowers her head,
I breathe in the scent of her favorite jasmine hair oil.
My eyes flood with tears
at that moment.
I wipe them away without anybody noticing.

After putting on three shirts,
three pairs of pants, and a raincoat,
I look like a pregnant woman.

7 | THE JADE *KWUN YUM* PENDANT

Ah Mah comes in, unusually quiet.
She is keeping an eye on the door
in case the police come.
While *Ma* is taking a turn watching the door,
Ah Mah ties a jade *Kwun Yum* pendant
on a red string around my neck
to keep me safe on my journey.

I can't help but thrust my hands out to her
and weep
as her bony fingers touch my flesh.

Like an epidemic,
we all weep,
with tears
like water being released from a dam.

I wish I could just stay home.
I wish I could just forget the police.
I wish I could just forget taking care of my brothers.
I wish I could just forget *Baba*
and stay
with *Ma* and *Ah Mah*.

But I can't.

My distant cousin,
who is driving us to the countryside
in his cargo scooter,
is waiting
about two blocks away.

8 | DEPARTURE

Fearing the police on the street might discover our secret,
Daigo and *Dee Dee* leave the house first.
I follow ten minutes later
without looking back to wave at *Ma* and *Ah Mah*.

We pretend we're going to visit
our *pau pau* in the countryside.

We all memorize
Pau Pau's address
in case we get stopped on the street
and are asked where we are going.

I dash into the scooter.
None of us talk,
not even *Dee Dee*.
My brain feels like a sheet of blank white paper
as the three-wheeled scooter,
with us sitting in the cargo compartment
behind the driver,
bumps and twists
and sends my city,
my hometown,
retreating backward
until we get to the wide-open country fields.

The scooter bounces up and down
hour after hour.
It lulls us to sleep.
Then, suddenly, a bump
and it stops.
We get out of the scooter.
Cousin points to a shed far from the road
where we have to go.
He wishes us luck
and drives off quickly.

The rain stopped long ago.
We stumble along a narrow path,
with our sandals and feet sinking into the soft mud,
for what seems like half an hour
toward a shed
in the middle of the wilderness,
outside of the city of My Tho.

Many people are already there,
milling around in the shed.
Some sleep;
some smoke;
some talk,
while babies cry

and children play hide-and-seek.

A man checks our names
and tells us to sit down and wait.
We sit on the ground at a dry spot in the shed
and sleep through the night.
The next day
we eat our food and wait
all day.

9 | THE RAID

On the night of the next day, May 11, 1979,
the same man announces quietly,
"Time to board the boat.
Be quiet, but quick."

Daigo holds *Dee Dee*'s hand
and I walk next to them,
pressed on all sides by many people,
all rushing,
tramping through the weeds
without worrying about snakes.

We pass the dark bushes around us
and move toward the open sea
without making a sound,
except for
the shuffle of hasty footsteps.

Someone suddenly shouts, "Police!"
People start to run,
like birds
fleeing
from a cage that is suddenly opened.
People scream.
People cry.

I hear *Dee Dee* cry.
I hear *Dee Dee* call *"Daigo!"* from behind me.

I turn for him,
but the crowd stands like a wall:
so tall,
so thick,
so powerful.
It pushes me back all the way
into something that
wobbles.

10 | WANTING TO GO HOME

I find myself in a sampan
with about ten shadows sitting in it.
I call out to my brothers,
but do not hear them respond.
I want to get out of the boat.
The person next to me pushes me down.
The boatman curses me
as he starts rowing
desperately along the shore.

I am frightened
without *Daigo* and *Dee Dee*.
I want the boat to stop.
I want to go back home.

The boatman ignores me.
The boat slips into the thick reeds.
The boatman orders,
"All of you duck your heads down and
don't make a sound.
There are patrol boats everywhere."

A baby starts to cry.
The mother shoves her nipple into the baby's mouth,
and the baby quiets down.

A man in front of me keeps looking back.
Then I see the shadows of two sampans
also hiding among the reeds.

Are my brothers in these sampans?
I wonder.

11 | PATROL BOAT?

I hear a muffled sound
from the shadow of a big boat that
cruises close to the shore.
My heart tightens.
Is it a patrol boat?

The boatman holds up lighted incense sticks.
He waves them up and down
several times
toward the big shadow that has no lights.

What does that mean? I wonder until
our boatman quickly paddles toward the big shadow,
which has responded with tiny dots of light
waving up and down
a few times.

"I don't want to go!" I protest.
"Shut up!" the boatman demands.
Our boat reaches the big shadow.
"Hurry, board the boat," the boatman commands.
Someone from the big boat pulls people up,
while the boatman boosts them up from behind.
Our boat wobbles
like a metal plate

dropped onto a tile floor.

I push his hand away
as the boatman tries to raise me up.
I cry, "I can't find my brothers!
I'm not going!"
The man in the big boat says in a low voice,
"They might be in the sampans behind."

So I let him pull me up into the boat.

Another man stuffs something into my hand and says,
"If you want to throw up,
do it in the bag.
Go down below."

I follow the one in front of me
down narrow steps
to the cabin beneath the deck.
Another man orders the newcomers,
"Squeeze to the back. Quick!"

12 | THE CABIN

The cabin,
the lowest place in the boat,
has no windows.
It is hot and smells of sweat,
mud,
and vomit.
I feel suffocated as soon as I step in.
There are two dim lights
hanging from the low ceiling.
Many people have already squeezed into the cabin
without making a sound.

There is not enough space.
I sit on the floor
with my knees touching my chin,
with no room to stretch my legs.
I can't see clearly if the persons
who sit around me
are men or women.

The lights in this low cabin finally go off.
The sound of the boat that is beginning to head out
is muffled.
Someone has covered the engine
to avoid being heard

by a patrol boat.

For me,
there is no way back.
I am scared.
I am alone,
like a kite
that has broken away from its string and
doesn't know
where it will
land.

I weep
with my hand covering my mouth.

13 | I AM SO SICK

The boat bobs up and down,
like a fishing cork on the surface of the water
when a fish nibbles the bait.
The sound of people vomiting
breaks the quiet night
now and then,
and the nauseating smell
makes me want to stop breathing.

I throw up, too.
The force of my vomit explosion
soils the back of the person who sits in front of me.
He curses.

Liquid drips on top of my head
from someone who has urinated
on the upper deck
without bothering to go to the toilet.
But I am too sick to scold whoever did it.

14 | LOOKING FOR LOVED ONES

I am awakened by the sound of mumbling.
It is dawn.
Tiny light beams filter through cracks from above.
Many flashlights shine on every face,
and names are called out everywhere.
More than ten families are looking
for their missing loved ones.

I call out for *Dee Dee* and *Daigo*
while some people loudly recount
their stories of being raided by the police.

Babies are crying;
small kids are scared and restless.
The whole cabin is as noisy as
a market.

15 | BREAKFAST

A sailor hands us
a big bowl of plain rice porridge
for breakfast.
He tells us to sip it and then
give it to the one sitting next to us.

The porridge is so bitter that
I take only one sip.
Many spit it out, complaining,
"This heartless sailor
used sea water to make porridge."

We can go to the toilet,
but we are not allowed to go up to the deck.
The Vietnamese patrol boats can stop us
if they spot us.

When they leave their seats,
people ask those next to them to save their seats.
I don't care about my seat.
Finding my brothers is more important
than saving my seat.
I call out my brothers' names while
squeezing through the crowd
toward the toilet.

I hear a tiny whimper
as I come back.
My heart accelerates, and
I follow the cry,
which comes from underneath the steps.
I am about to trip over an old lady
who sits near the steps when I call,
"Dee Dee!"

I throw myself onto him.
We both break into loud wails,

as if we have been apart for a long time.
"Where is *Daigo*?" I ask him.

"I don't know."

"Wasn't *Daigo* holding your hand
when we walked toward the boat?"

"He was. But someone grabbed him from nowhere.
He let go of my hand and told me to find you.
But people pushed me.
I fell down.
I grabbed someone's leg and didn't let go."

At this moment,
I don't feel sorry for myself.
I don't have any fear
of going to a place that is unknown,
alone.

At this moment,
I am *Dee Dee*'s *daigo*;
I am *Dee Dee*'s *baba*;
I am *Dee Dee*'s *ma* and *ah mah*;
I am *Dee Dee*'s sister;

I am *Dee Dee*'s everything.

At this moment,
I swear
I accept responsibility for my brother,
even though I am only eleven.

I say to him,
"Don't be scared.
You have me.
I have you.
We are together.
We are okay."

17 | *DAIGO*'S FATE

"Why did the police grab *Daigo*?" *Dee Dee* asks.
"Why didn't they grab me?'

"I don't know.
I heard they grabbed others, too."

"Will he be okay?"

"Yes. They will send him to jail,
like others they have arrested.
Ma and *Ah Mah* will bail him out.
He will be okay.
He is strong."

"How do you know he will be okay?"

"I didn't have a bad dream about him.
Did you?"

Dee Dee shakes his head.

"That means he is okay," I assure him.

He whispers,
"I peed in my pants."

I would have laughed at him back home.
But I squeeze his hand and say,
"Who cares? Someone peed on my head last night."

I help him take off his extra clothing
and tie all of it into a pouch.
I abandon my own seat.
Together
we squeeze underneath the steps.

I can breathe in the fresh air.
I can see a patch of sky.
And I know
we are going to be okay.

18 | THEY BREAK THEIR PROMISE

No meal is served for the rest of the day—
just water
and the salty, watery porridge.
People complain,
for they were promised
there would be three meals a day
when they paid the steep fee.

Dee Dee is hungry.
He drinks the water
and eats the food we brought with us.

I drink a couple of sips of water
but eat only one cracker.
I am afraid that
I will throw up if I eat any more.

19 | SOUTH CHINA SEA

On the morning of the third day,
the small Vietnamese captain tells us that
we have finally reached international waters.
We are now in the South China Sea.

We cheer the welcome news.
"We are free now!" someone shouts.
"The Communists have no right to arrest us
anymore!" another remarks.
"We can breathe easily now!" an old man says.

Dee Dee and I follow some people going up on deck,
while many older people remain where they are,
afraid they will lose their seats.

It is so good to stretch out my legs.
It is so good to breathe the fresh air.
It is so good to see the dome-like blue sky.
It is so good to see the dark blue water—
so calm, so beautiful.

And it is so good
to finally feel free.

We all gaze far away,
where the water kisses the end of the sky,
to search for the location of Vietnam,
hoping to have a last glimpse of our homeland.

Some say it is there,
and some say it's in the opposite direction.
But the ocean looks like a round table,
and our homeland could be in any direction.

Then
we all fall into silence.
Perhaps
we all have mixed feelings.

I am sad, as I look far, far away
beyond the edge of the sky.
I still remember how
Ma held tightly on to my hands
and wasn't willing to let me go.
Ah Mah tried to hurry me to go,
but she was still clinging to me
and giving me last-minute instructions on
how to keep myself healthy.

Now,
I haven't gone far away,
but
I miss my family;
I miss my home
already.
Can I ever go back?

My eyes are drowning, like the waves
rolling in,
flooding,
then spilling
down.

"I want to go home," *Dee Dee* says quietly.
I can't comfort him.
I would burst out wailing
if I just said a word.

21 | A GOOD LUCK SIGN

Someone on the deck cries,
"Look—some big fish are jumping!"

"Where?" the silent people awake, as if
retreating from their homesickness.

"Wait—they will jump again."

We wait.

"There! See!"

We applaud
as we see two big gray creatures
leap up,
like gleaming silvery arches
against the blue sky.
Their bodies throw droplets of white spray
into the air,
and then they plunge back into the water
with a big splash.

We forget the sadness
and look forward to seeing them jump up
again.

Dee Dee asks,
"What kind of fish are they?"
A boy next to us replies,
"They are sharks."

A city-looking person corrects him in Vietnamese,
declaring,
"No, they are not sharks, Nam."

Another chimes in, "Maybe they are whales."

A sailor with rotten teeth says,
"They are dolphins.
A sign of good luck."

"How?" we ask.

"They are following us," the sailor says.
"They will bring us luck."

A sign of hope,
like a colorful rainbow
arching across the sky
after a rain.

22 | PIRATES

Dee Dee and Nam, who can speak Cantonese,
become friends.
They play pirates.

Dee Dee says to me,
"We are pirates, and you are the oarsman."
He puts one hand over his eye,
like pirates we saw in a comic book
with a patch covering an eye.
They stick out two fingers
as guns,
and they squeeze among the tightly packed adults
who are assembled in small groups
and declare that they will go to
whatever country will take them.

I wave both arms back and forth
like an oarsman does.
Several kids join us in our pirate play.
Dee Dee tells them to cover one eye,
and they all
chase one another on the deck,
until someone shouts,
"Pirates! Go back down!
Pirates!"

Dee Dee and Nam laugh,

"They are afraid of us.

They think we are—"

Someone screams and cries out shrilly in terror,

"Pirates! Pirates!"

23 | THE REAL PIRATES

A small fishing boat containing several men
is speeding toward us.
They hold up axes in the air and yell menacingly.
I grab *Dee Dee*'s arm
while Nam's *baba* hurries him back to the cabin below.
Other parents call their children's names.
Suddenly, the deck looks like
a trampled anthill,
with people scurrying toward the steps.

The captain asks all the men,
"Should we fight?
We have long knives, axes, and hammers in my cabin.
We will die for sure if we don't fight."

Many men, including Nam's *baba*, shout,
"Fight! Fight to the death!"
They all rush to the front of the deck
to go face-to-face with the approaching pirates.

Our boat tilts as the force of so many people
suddenly moving forward
makes the weight on the deck uneven.

Someone shouts from the top of the steps

to those of us below,
"Move toward the back of the cabin
to balance the weight!"

No one listens.
Several old ladies kneel on the floor,
crying and praying
in Cantonese and Vietnamese.
One old couple
still sits in the corner, unmoving.

A mother inserts something into her baby's diaper,
and the baby seems to know something is wrong
and starts crying.

An old man wraps up a small jar of coffee
and hides it underneath his armpit.
And I am thinking,
Who would care about your coffee?

An old lady in black urges a young woman
to take off her headband
and give it to her.
Apparently, something was sewn inside,
but it drops and rolls to the floor.

The old lady searches under someone's legs,
but an angry old man in blue shouts,
"What are you doing in this crisis?
Don't you know we all are about to be killed?"

A city-like lady
gets a big tube of toothpaste from her belongings
and orders Nam, "Hurry! Put this with your toothbrush."
I wonder if she has inserted rolled-up American money
inside the tube.
I have heard of people doing that before.

Next to them is a girl about my age
with a haircut like a boy.
She quickly smears something dark on her face
to appear less appealing to the pirates.

I have nothing to hide.
All the gold is in *Daigo*'s clothing.
Ma helped him sew the gold
inside the seam of his shirt.
Ma said that *Daigo* would be much better
at taking care of it.

I just hold on to *Dee Dee.*
But I can hear my teeth
chattering
as I fear what the pirates might do
besides robbing.

The girl hands me the small bag of black ash,
but my hands are shaking so much that
I almost drop it.
She helps me apply the ash
onto my face
and smiles at me,
as if assuring me that
I will be okay.

24 | OUR BOAT WILL SINK

Our boat will sink.
The back of it has gradually tilted up
while the front
has tilted down.
Many small children have been thrown
to the floor.
They scream.
They cry.

Someone shouts again,
"Move to the back!
The boat will sink!"

Everyone is still, like statues.
They fear they won't have anything to hold on to.
The old lady in black cries in Vietnamese,
"*Duc Me,* please don't let the boat sink!"

More people cry;
more people pray
to Buddha,
Kwun Yum,
the Heaven God,
or *Duc Me*
to save them.

Everybody seems to fear that
we will either be drowned
or killed
or raped
by the pirates
because we hear the shouting above,
"We will fight till we drop!"
and we hear the tramping
of desperate feet above.
We are afraid.
Are the pirates already on board?

Someone warns from the top of the steps,
"Young women and girls, find places to hide!
They are less than fifty feet away!"

The cabin looks like a war zone
after a devastating strike.
People begin moving hither and thither,
trying to find places to hide.
But there are not many places to hide.
Some cry and wail that
they prefer drowning to being
raped.

I cry, and *Dee Dee* cries even louder.

I don't want to die.

I don't want to be raped.

I want to go home.

I want to be with *Ma* and *Ah Mah,*

who can embrace me and protect me.

25 | SOMEONE SHOUTS FROM ABOVE

The whole cabin sounds like
people in mourning.

Someone announces from above,
“Hooray! The pirate boat has gone!
Hooray! The pirate boat has gone!”

We are bewitched.
We look at one another
and can’t decide if it is true,
until
we hear clapping,
until
the small Vietnamese captain comes down
and announces that
we are okay.

Our quick-witted captain
unscrewed a light bulb
in the pilot house
and aimed it at the pirate boat,
which was less than fifteen feet away from us.
They thought it was a grenade
and sped away!

Many people give thanks
to the quick-thinking captain.
Many old ladies kneel down in front of him,
"Oh, praise be! *Kwun Yum* and *Duc Me* have saved us.
The captain has saved us!"

The humble captain thanks them and says,
"We are glad that we chased them away
without any bloodshed
and without damaging our boat.
We hope we won't encounter more pirates."

Back home we had heard that
after pirates robbed the people on boats,
they would sabotage the engine
so the boat couldn't continue.
They would radio other pirates to come for that boat.
That's why sometimes a boat could be robbed
three or four times
if they were unlucky.

I hope our boat
will not be that one.

Our boat starts going again
after the captain warns that
no one should use flashlights
or smoke on deck
after dark.
The lights might easily be seen
by the pirates, even from a distance.

People are more submissive than before.
They heed the warnings of the captain.
As night falls,
the whole cabin is as dark as
a cave, deep down in the earth.
No one complains.

Instead, more volunteers go up on the deck
to stand watch,
while those still in the cabin
continue talking about the close call.
They still praise the humble, quick-witted captain.

27 | THE DEAD BODY

Someone complains
that there is a smell like that of a decaying corpse
coming from the back of the cabin.
Someone has died.

Angry voices, shooting like flying swords,
protest.
"Throw the body into the water!"
"They are selfish! That person must
have been dead for some time,
but they wanted to cover it up!"
"No wonder they have been glued there
even though the pirates came!"

An old lady cries and begs in Cantonese,
"Please, *please* don't throw my niece into the sea.
Please let us bury her on dry land."

A couple of men try to grab the body.
The old lady threatens,
"If you throw my niece into the ocean,
I will jump in with her!"

A sailor comes.
He shines a flashlight onto the angry passengers

who are all covering their noses,
squeezing away from the old couple, who are isolated.
The old lady guards the body
while the old man stands up,
ready to fight if necessary.

The old lady cries to the sailor,
"Please have mercy on this young lady
who died so young. . . ."

The sailor retreats without saying a word.
He returns carrying the captain's words—
to let them remove the body onto the deck
and wait until they reach dry land to bury her.

The angry voices calm down.
The old couple are so pleased.
They say the captain will have good fortune
because of his kindness.

So the sailor throws a big piece of plastic sheet
to the couple.
The old lady weeps.
Together with the old man
they wrap the body carefully.

They carry the body
with difficulty.

Nobody offers to help them,
but everyone watches
as if the old couple are contagious.

Nam's *baba* finally
gives them a hand.

The couple stay on the deck,
despite the rain,
despite the burning sun,
and despite occasional high winds and waves,
to guard the body.

Yet, their seats at the back of cabin
remain empty.

28 | SO QUIET, LIKE DEATH

I have lost track
of how many days and nights
we have been on the ocean.
I am glad we haven't encountered
any ferocious storms.

All I know is that
the sailors have stopped serving porridge.
The water they serve now looks like it has green algae in it.
Dee Dee and I just carefully drink a few sips.

I am glad I seldom throw up now.
I haven't had much water or food.
I seldom need to go to the bathroom,
but when I go,
there is hardly any urine.
The little that comes out is a dark golden color.
I don't feel like standing up
or talking to *Dee Dee*.
I just feel very sleepy.

A baby cries.
The sound is so weak, like a kitten meowing.
The mother doesn't have milk for him,
even though she sticks her nipple into his mouth.

A pregnant woman sobs.
She worries her fetus has no nourishment.

At last, the sailors stop giving us water—
not even the water with green algae in it.
There is no more water.

Our cabin is so quiet now,
like death.
People just sleep;
even the small children;
even the babies.

29 | LAND!

At last, a man shouts
from the top of the steps:
"We see birds!
We are going to see land soon!"

The passengers suddenly come alive
again,
as though suddenly given nourishment
after a long fast.
They ask, "What country is it?"

Someone snaps,
"Who cares what country it is
as long as it is land!"
The old people start giving thanks to their gods.

Despite my weakness,
I hold on to *Dee Dee,* and together with the others,
go up to see.

It is barely dawn.
Far away, there is a gray arch of shadow,
like a camel's back,
half-hidden in the mist,
on the far horizon.

I suddenly feel so strong

that I can stand against the wind.

My eyes cloud over

as I stare at the faraway shadow.

30 | PIRATES ONCE AGAIN

Everyone's face is as bright as a morning sunflower,
for our ordeal will end
soon.
Then someone spots a dot far away.
It is moving.
It is getting bigger.
And it is speeding up
toward us.

It is a boat!

The person warns,
"Pirates! More pirates!"

We scramble down to the cabin like a disaster
is going to strike
again.
The whole cabin turns upside down once more.
We cry,
we scream,
we pray,
we hide
until
a sailor says,
"It is not a pirate boat!

It is a fishing boat!
We are saved."

Someone asks, "From what country?"
Several voices cut in,
"Who cares from what country?"

The sailor assures, "We are saved."

"Five days! Finally."
Nam's parents and other adults all
let out a sigh of relief.
Dee Dee and Nam and other children jump up and down.
Dao, Nam's sister who applied the ash to my face, cheers.
I cheer, and I shout.
And the old ladies are giving thanks,
kneeling down on the floor.

Goodbye, uncertainty.
Welcome, the new land!

31 | OUR SINCERE THANKS

As the engine of our boat stops,
the sailor with rotten teeth
comes down and asks,
"Can anyone speak English?
Our captain needs help."

Nam's *baba* says,
"Just a little."
He goes up with the sailor.

In a minute,
Nam's *baba* returns and says,
"Good news!
These fishermen are going to take us
to the refugee camp."

Some teens raise up two fingers
in a V for victory
while the others' faces beam.

"But . . . ," Nam's *baba* continues,
"they want us to give them
gold or watches in return
for the gas and their effort."
Not a single person objects.

Someone says,
"Using our treasure to prevent a disaster!"

Another says, "They are our saviors!
I don't mind using some of my gold
to save our whole family!"

A man says,
"Nothing is more precious than
being put onto land!"

Dee Dee whispers,
"Why do they want gold?
Why don't they want money?"
I say,
"Our money is only good in Vietnam.
Gold can be used anywhere."

So the whole group of passengers springs into action,
as a sailor holds out two big serving bowls,
the ones used for serving porridge,
to collect the donations.

They put in
gold rings,

a gold pendant,
a gold bracelet,
a gold necklace,
even
a heavy gold bangle.

The man who has the coffee jar puts it
into the bowl.
The sailor says,
"Give them gold, not coffee."

The man takes a ring
hidden in the seam of his clothing
and places it into the bowl.

Nam's *ma* puts in a pair of earrings and a ring
without any hesitation.
Teenagers who don't have much gold
take off their watches to add to the bowl.

Dee Dee murmurs,
"What are *we* giving them?
Daigo has all the gold."

I untie the red string and

give them the jade *Kwun Yum*.
I am sure *Ah Mah* wouldn't mind
me giving it away
if it ends up saving our lives.
But the sailor skips me by saying,
"They only want gold and watches."

There are two big bowls full of treasure,
which dazzle my eyes.
The fishermen are happy.
We are happy.

32 | SAILING TO THE LAND

The fishermen tie two thick ropes
to either side of our boat.
They begin to tow us
to the refugee camp.

Everyone's spirits are high,
for our ordeal is going to be over.
The lights in our cabin are turned back on.
No more worries about pirates.

As people are relaxing,
I quietly tell my family in my mind,
I am sorry I haven't thought of you for days.
Now we are safe.
We are going to land soon.
Don't worry about Dee Dee *and me.*

The journey seems endless.
It has been almost a day and a night.
Some people are restless, complaining,
"Why does it take so long
to get to the refugee camp?
Didn't we just see land?"

Another says,

"Don't worry,
as long as we are being towed by the fishermen."

It makes sense.
Some go back to sleep.
Others quietly talk about their lives back home.

On the second day before dawn,
we are awakened by a strange sound
followed by a sudden dipping of our boat.
"What's happening?"
We are suddenly alert.

33 | THE OUTRAGE

A sailor reports angrily
at the top of the steps,
"Can you believe that?
They towed us back
into international waters,
and then they cut the ropes and sped away!
They said they changed their minds
and hope someone else will pick us up!"

The whole boat is as furious as
bubbles from boiling water
about to spill out.

They ask,
"Where are we now? We have been cheated!"

They yell,
"How could they do such an inhumane thing!"

They curse,
"Those tricky fishermen will die in a terrible way!"

They wonder,
"Were they really fishermen?
Or were they pirates disguising themselves

as fishermen?"

They argue,
"We don't even know what country they belong to!"

"That's why I asked what country they were from,
and you all jumped on me."

Some fight back.
"What difference does it make if they were from
Hong Kong, Japan, Malaysia, the Philippines,
or some other country?"

It is the calm captain who puts out the fire
when he says,
"I am sorry.
Maybe they were a group of pirates or rebels
from some unknown country.
But what is done is done.
We were all desperate
to get off the water onto dry land.
But we will continue to sail
until we find land.
We will land at the first place we see
before our fuel completely runs out."

The voices die down.

I feel a chill all over
as I hear the word "pirate."
I am so glad I didn't give them my jade *Kwun Yum*
after all.

PART TWO

May 18, 1979
Somewhere in Malaysia

34 | THE MORNING OF THE EIGHTH DAY

On the morning of the eighth day
after we left our homeland,
we reach an unknown bay.
No one asks or cares what country the bay belongs to,
for we are tired and short of energy.
But we are still alive.

"At last!" everyone cheers,
and the sound of raucous clapping is as loud as
a string of firecrackers going off
at the opening of a new store.

The captain suggests,
"Since we do not know where we are,
and in case we are forced to leave the bay,
let's disable our boat
before we leave,
so no one can send us out to sea again."

"Yes!" everybody agrees,
and they take action right away.
The adults and teens use the axes and knives that
they took out to fight the pirates
to chop here and there
except where the corpse is located.

The captain and others crowd
into the pilot house to sabotage
the engine.

Small children like *Dee Dee* and Nam
jump up,
trying to break the deck,
glad to be free from their long confinement.

They are thinking that breaking
the deck could make the boat sink.

I am very weak.
Still, I join with other girls
using just one foot to stamp on the deck,
but the boards don't break.

The boat is alive with
the excitement of destruction,
joy, and hope,
and then the captain announces,
"The engine no longer works!
The boat can't travel anymore!"

Everybody declares,

"The ordeal is over!
No one can trick us anymore!"
The old ladies drop onto the deck
and give thanks.

35 | THE HORROR

The five sailors tie several long ropes
onto the boat
and throw them into the water
before they jump from the boat.
They grab the ropes and pull them all the way
to the shore.
Some young men can't wait.
They jump after the sailors
and swim to the beach.

They give the sailors a hand
when they try to pull the boat
closer to the shore.

When one sailor commands, "One, two, three!"
more than thirty men,
some of them in the surf,
pull with all their might,
like in a fiercely contested tug-of-war.

They rest a few seconds and pull again.
They pull many times.
Each time is entertainment for us
until the boat can't progress anymore.
It comes to rest on the seabed.

It is now about two hundred feet
from the shore.
The sailors secure the ropes to palm trees
that surround the beach.

The captain throws many wooden buckets
into the water.

The sailors tie the buckets onto the ropes,
about every ten feet, all the way to the shore.
When the sailors urge the people
to jump from the boat,
the old lady in black cries,
"I'll drown for sure
if I have to go into the water!"

The pregnant woman wails,
"Jumping into the water will harm my baby,"
while her husband tries hard to convince her.

I feel like I am going to have diarrhea.
Dee Dee and I do not know how to swim.
Looking from the deck to the water below
it appears very deep.
I can't see the bottom.

My legs feel like cooked rice noodles,
just looking at the water below.

The sailors and the young men
who are treading water
convince us to jump.
They say,
"All you have to do is jump into the water
and hold on to the ropes.
The ropes will guide you to the shore!"

I am thinking,
It is easier said than done.

But *Dee Dee* claps,
"Let's jump!
I am sick of staying on this boat
for so long!"

"No! We will wait for them to help us!"

But he jumps into the water.
I am horrified. I scream.
I jump in after him.
I must save my brother.

36 | THE RESCUE

Water gushes into my nose and mouth.
I panic.
I kick.
I reach out with my arms,
but I can't find the rope
no matter how frantically I move my arms.

Someone grabs me.
I latch on to him for dear life.
My head is suddenly out of the water.
I cough and choke in spasms.
Water comes out from my mouth and nose,
as the man drags me
all the way
onto the shore.

I hear someone curse me
for not waiting for the crew members.
I cough and start to sob at the same time,
but I am alert.

Where is my brother?

37 | MY DECISION

Nam's *baba*, soaking wet, is holding *Dee Dee*'s hand.
When he sees me,
Dee Dee lets go of Nam's *baba*'s hand
and runs to me.
I slap him in the face
and scold him, "Why didn't you listen to me!
You almost got me drowned!"

He cries.

Nam's *baba* asks me in Cantonese if I am okay.
I thank him for helping *Dee Dee*.
I am surprised that
he can speak Cantonese
without any accent.

Back home,
our family hardly ever mingled
with Vietnamese.
We had our own small quarter,
like an invisible wall that separated us
from the outside world.
We went to Chinese schools;
we ate Chinese food;
we spoke Chinese;

we practiced
traditional Chinese medicine and customs.

But now I have changed my mind.
I wish we could have been closer
to the Vietnamese
when I was at home.

People are still jumping off the boat.
Kids are jumping without any fear.
Many adults hold their noses
and close their eyes
before they jump.
Some say a prayer, then leap into the water.
Reluctant passengers sit on the edge of the boat
before pushing themselves off.
Others lie on their stomachs over the side of the boat
with their feet toward the water
and gradually move their legs downward,
then let go.

So
the bay resounds with the noise of
water splashing,
crying,
screaming,
and laughing for joy,
like a live orchestra performing
without a conductor.

But the elderly and young mothers,
including the pregnant woman,
are afraid to jump.

The captain secures a rope to the boat
and ties it underneath the young mothers' arms,
while they hold their screaming babies or toddlers.

He and their husbands carefully lower the mothers
down to the water,
where the people below retrieve them
and help them hold on to the ropes
and accompany them all the way to the shore.

The pregnant woman and the older people
are assisted safely to shore,
except for the old lady in black,
who refuses to be tied underneath her arms,
no matter how much her children beg her.
So she is the last one off the boat.
Her screams and cries sound like a pig
being slaughtered.

It takes a long time
before all the people are off the boat,
including the corpse that was on the deck.

Hooray!
We have ended our eight days on the water.

Of more than two hundred people,

no one drowns;

no one gets injured getting off the boat.

The captain is pleased.

We are pleased.

39 | INVESTIGATION

We are lying on the sandy shore
like dead fish.
The earth
is still rocking
beneath us
like a boat,
up and down.

The sailors bring the cooking utensils
and the people's belongings,
floating them to shore
on a large wooden hatch cover.

We search in the soaking wet pile.
Dee Dee finds his sandals.
I lost one of mine
when I was in the water.

Both *Dee Dee* and Nam are overjoyed.
Dee Dee asks if
he and Nam can play together again.

Dao and I nod and smile.
The charcoal on her face is almost gone.
Only a few traces of it remain.

I think mine is probably the same.

Her mother says to me gently in Cantonese,
with a heavy Vietnamese accent,
"We will stay together."

It touches me so much.
It is what I wanted.
Dee Dee and I will have a shoulder
to lean on
during this journey.

And I decide, from now on,
Dee Dee and I will address them as
Uncle and Auntie
for respect
and a sense of closeness.

Someone shouts from behind us.

Several soldiers suddenly appear
from nowhere
with their guns pointing at us.
We all let out a cry.
What country

are we in?

Dee Dee grabs my hand
fearfully.
I hold his hand in a tense grip.
Have we become criminals?

A tall soldier yells in English.
Uncle says, "They want us to return to our boat."

Murmurs rise among us.
"Tell them our boat doesn't work!"

The tall soldier is angry.
He wants to know
who sabotaged the boat.

We feel threatened.
They approach
with their guns still pointing at us.

I smell blood.

Some small children cry.
I hold my breath.

I can feel *Dee Dee,*
who is hiding behind me,
trembling.
He also participated in damaging the boat.

No one says a word.
Only the babies cry.
"Who is the captain?"
Uncle translates the tall soldier's question.

Our captain comes out from the crowd,
and he replies, "I am the captain."

The soldier asks him,
"Who participated in sabotaging the boat?"

The captain doesn't answer.

Everybody is breathless.

All the soldiers circle around us
with watchful eyes on our faces.

I can hear my heart thumping.
I fear:

Will they question us one by one,
like the police did back home?

We are all glued to the ground.
Nobody moves a bit.
If there was a fly,
we could hear it
humming by.

A shorter soldier mumbles something
to the tall soldier,
who orders all our men to stick out their hands.
Then they check our men's hands
one by one.

I am in a fog.
What does it mean? I wonder.
Without saying a word,
the taller soldier strikes the captain across the head
with the butt of his rifle.

We all let out a collective cry.
We are terrified.
Children start crying
in fear.

The soldier's gun comes down
onto the captain's head
once more.
He falls onto the sand.
Blood trickles down from his head.
He looks half dead.

I turn my head away

and cover *Dee Dee*'s eyes.
I hear the captain moan.
No one would dare to help him,
not even his own family.

Everybody is afraid.

The tall soldier is ready to hit him again.
A cry comes from the crowd,
"Stop it! Stop beating him!"
The old lady whose niece died drags herself
toward the soldier.
"Tell them!
Tell them our captain has a kind heart.
Tell them our captain let our niece stay on the deck
instead of throwing her into the water after she died.
Tell them, tell them!"

I don't know if the solider understands her,
for the lady uses her own body to block the captain
from the taller soldier.

"Are you all right?" the old lady asks the captain,
whose face is covered with blood and sand.
"Why did they only beat you up, but not any others?"

"Maybe they saw the black oil on my hands,"
the captain replies.

The lady tries to get him up.
The lady's husband comes up.
Uncle comes up.
Together,
they carry the captain
to a shady area where he can rest,
away from the sun.
His family comes to him.
The sailors come to him.

Within half an hour,
two soldiers accompany the captain to the hospital.
His family is very pleased.
The old lady concludes,
"At least they still have a conscience."

41 | THE WARNING

The soldiers record our names,
genders,
and nationalities,
as well as family units.
They warn us not to wander around
but to stay on this beach.
They say they will shoot
if any of us tries to escape.

I still have no idea
where we are.
Some say we have landed in Malaysia.
Some say we have landed in Indonesia.
Some say, "Who cares where we have landed?"

The ropes connected to our boat
have long been untied.
Eventually, our boat has drifted farther away.
People say it is a good sign.
No one will miss it.
No one will use it.

The sailors dig a big hole in the sand
to cook the rice
with salty water.
We share the same bowls again.
I eat only a bite;
Dee Dee eats two bites.

The old lady in black complains
about the salty rice.
The sailor fights back,
"You cook if you can find fresh water!"
The old lady in black keeps quiet.

43 | WATER

In the late afternoon,
someone says
he has discovered a deserted swimming pool nearby,
and there is still a little water in it.
We all swarm there.
Uncle's family, *Dee Dee,* and I follow the other people.
We go through some coconut trees,
still feeling like
we are rocking in the open sea.

When we see a small amount of water
in the lowest end of the abandoned pool,
all our spirits pick up.
Except for *Dee Dee*'s.
He is tense, hiding behind me,
afraid of being seen by the two soldiers
who are guarding us with guns in their hands.

Uncle notices.
He whispers to *Dee Dee,*
"Don't be afraid.
They won't harm you."

Dee Dee whispers back,
"What if they find out

I tried to mess up the boat?
They won't beat me up like the captain
was beat up by the mean soldier?"

"No.
They won't beat you up.
Not every soldier is mean.
They are just trying to keep us in order."

Dee Dee then
comes out from behind me
but still keeps an eye on the soldiers.

The water looks green,
and there are tiny wormlike mosquito larvae in it.
My lips turn down in disappointment.
Uncle says to us,
"Drink it anyway.
You need water to survive."

I feel chilled
as I scoop up a handful of water
and see there are tiny brownish creatures
swimming inside my palm.
I don't think I can do it.

Uncle says,
"Just close your eyes and drink it."

I force myself
to swallow two sips of water.
It is cool and energizing,
despite the tiny creatures;
despite the pain and blood from my cracked lips.

And I tell *Dee Dee* to do the same.

We leave the pool quickly
to make room for the latecomers.
A couple of sailors carry a bucket of water
for the other people who can't come.

Dee Dee is not harmed by the soldiers.
He waves at them
when we are leaving.
Surprisingly,
one nods and
the other one smiles.

44 | THE FIRST NIGHT

We find places
underneath palm trees for shelter.

We hang our damp clothes
across nearby shrubs.
The pleasant wind is strong
and feels good.
It dries our clothes in no time,
but it leaves white lines of salt as souvenirs.

The grown-ups do not talk.
The children do not play.
We are exhausted
and lie on the sand
with a piece of plastic as our bedsheet.
We are so pleased
that we are safely on land.

Dee Dee falls fast asleep right next to me,
but I can't sleep,
even though I can stretch out my legs.

Looking at the big moon half hiding
behind the palm trees,
I think about my family back home.

Are they already in bed?
I want to tell *Ma* and *Ah Mah*
we have met a noble family;
I want to tell them *Daigo* could be in jail;
I want to tell them I miss
their homemade wontons,
the freshly cooked rice,
and the vegetables we have
at every meal.
I want to tell them
many, many things,
until
I can't see the moon.
I can't hear the strong wind.

45 | THE RED CROSS, OUR SAVIOR

I am awakened
by the noise of engines the next morning.
So are *Dee Dee* and Uncle's family.
We are uncertain
what is going on
until
we see six people come out from some trucks,
with Red Cross armbands
wrapped around
their upper arms.

We cheer.
Our saviors are finally here.
We heard back home
that Red Cross workers are good people and
that they have kind hearts.
We feel safe when we see them.

They tell us to form six lines.
Each worker is in charge of one line.
They distribute a bag full of food to everyone,
even to a tiny baby.
I feel like I am getting *lai see* from *Ah Mah*
on Chinese New Year.

Inside the bag
is a five-day supply of food:
rice,
tea bags,
coffee,
crackers,
canned sardines,
canned curry chicken,
canned beans,
and instant noodles.
We even get toilet paper!

Everyone starts to eat,
either with fingers
or with two thin twigs as chopsticks.

Like a starved prisoner,
I greedily stuff crackers and sardines
into my mouth.
I taste the blood from my cracked-open lips;
I taste the salty tears
streaming down my cheeks.

Sometime later,
the Red Cross trucks drive away with

the pregnant lady
and a sick little girl,
whose mother accompanies her
to the hospital.

The workers and a soldier
help bury the old couple's niece.
The old lady is so sad,
but she is very pleased that
her niece has a dry place to rest.

And Uncle finds out from the Red Cross worker
that we are standing on Malaysian soil.

46 | GOING TO A REFUGEE CAMP

We obey the rule
not to wander away.
We rest in the shade
all day
to restore our energy
and wait
to be sent to a refugee camp.

While the children,
even *Dee Dee* and Nam,
pee and do their job anywhere they please,
we hide among the thick trees
away from the others to relieve ourselves
or change clothes
after a sponge bath.

The third day,
several big buses come
to take us to a refugee camp.
We cry, "Finally!"
and applaud,
while the old ladies drop down
and give thanks.

We get into the buses by groups.

I make sure *Dee Dee* and I
are in the same group
with Uncle and his family.

"Are we going to America now?"
Dee Dee asks as we get into the bus.

"No," Uncle says.
"We have to wait for a while
in the refugee camp."

"Why?"

"There are so many people and
so many things they have to prepare."

The bus, which has two soldiers
sitting in the front with guns,
travels down a paved road.

There are huge rubber tree plantations
and tall palm trees on both sides.
A couple of dark, tanned workers
are cutting the palm seeds
with long bamboo poles.

The land is green and lush and peaceful,
like my home
used to be.

47 | THE PLACE WE ARE GOING TO SETTLE

The soldiers guard us
as we walk down a narrow dirt path
into a wooded area
where other refugees,
about three or four hundred,
have already camped.

They have made "houses"
by constructing frameworks
of sticks
and covering them with
grass mats.

Others have just used plastic sheets on top of the sticks
with other plastic sheets on the ground
as their simple beds.

Colorful clothes hang everywhere
on ropes between the trees.

Children are running around
while the grown-ups sit in small groups talking,
sipping tea,
drinking coffee, or
smoking.

They raise their heads and smile,
as if saying, “I am glad you made it.”

So here is the place we are going to settle.

I do as Uncle and Auntie do.
We look for a space that is flat and dry.
We pull out the dead, scattered weeds
with our bare hands.
We ignore the ants and bugs crawling all around us.
We break off long green saplings
in the woods.
We make four holes in the ground
and insert the four saplings for the frame.
We tie the corners of my plastic sheet on top of the saplings
for the roof.
We spread out *Dee Dee*'s sheet on the ground
as our bed.
I say,
"I call it our
'House Without Walls.'"

Dee Dee and Nam cheer.
"We like the name—House Without Walls."

49 | GETTING INFORMATION

Uncle goes around
to get information
regarding the interview
from the ones who have been here already.

Back home
we heard that all the boat people,
like us now,
would have the same goal—
the same anxious desire—
to be interviewed
so their names would be on the waiting list.
They hoped that someone would sponsor them
to start a new life
in their new land.

When Uncle comes back,
he tells us that this is just a temporary camp
and that we need to get into the regular camp
before we can be interviewed.
So we need to be patient.

He warns Dao and me,
"They said some men
have been bothering the young girls.

You go to the latrine together
and never go alone."

He also finds out
there is a man
who will come once in a while
to help us purchase our necessities,
but with gold only.

My heart tightens.

Dee Dee cries,
"We don't have any gold!
What should we do?"

Uncle assures us
we can share their essentials.
He just signs up for what we need.
The goods will be here in a couple of days.

I thank him
from the bottom of my heart.

50 | THE STINKY LATRINES

The swiftly fabricated latrines
are about three hundred feet away from the campsite.
Yet the stinky smell has already welcomed us
in the breeze from far away.

There are two holes dug into the earth—
one for men
and one for women,
next to each other—
and they are shielded by woven dried grass mats.

There is a rule that
everybody should use the latrines,
and they are forbidden from toileting elsewhere,
including the children.
Whoever disobeys and is caught
must cover up the two holes
and dig two new ones
and separate them with mats
for the new latrines.

51 | THE FRESH, COLD WELL WATER

Uncle borrows a bucket from someone
who has already settled here.
We follow the narrow dirt path
made by the refugees
to a well
near a few houses on stilts.

People around the well are arguing
about someone breaking in line.
Two soldiers who are guarding us next to the well
do not interfere in the argument.
Uncle tries to settle the dispute
by letting the eldest ones
stay in the front of the line,
for not everyone had water to drink
after their meal.

The line quietens down.

Uncle shares the water he has drawn up
with us.
We scoop it with our hands
and drink it scoop after scoop,
because the water doesn't have any creatures in it
like before.

I never could have imagined
what a scoopful of fresh, cold well water
would do for me!

52 | THE FIRST NIGHT SLEEPING IN OUR HOUSE

The first night in the campsite is dark,
except for the soldiers
who are on duty in the shed
and a few early comers
who have flashlights.

We lie down carefully,
afraid our legs
will kick down the posts
of our "house without walls"
and cause the plastic roof
to collapse.

We use our raincoats as cover.
Auntie reminded me
that it would be chilly
in the middle of the night.

The mosquitoes buzz around our ears,
but we don't have any insect repellant
to chase them away.
Dee Dee complains.
I tell him,
"Look at the bright, round moon

and the stars around it
to distract you from the mosquitoes buzzing."

Dee Dee says,
"I want to go home.
This is no fun at all.
I don't like to eat the cold canned food.
It all has funny smells.
I want *Ah Mah* and *Ma*
to fix me Singapore noodles."

I say,
"I miss their food, too,
but we can't go back now.
Someday, we will be united again.
Right now, I just think about
seeing the snow and touching the snow.
You can think about
going to Walt Disney with *Baba*,
and you will feel
better."

"Will *Baba* recognize us?"

"Sure he will.

It has only been two years
since we last saw him.
Even if he can't recognize us,
we will recognize him."

Dee Dee is already sound asleep.

53 | THE CRY

I hear a sharp cry
while I am sound asleep,
"My face hurts so bad!"

"Why?" I ask.
In the light of dawn,
I see *Dee Dee* covering his left eye with his hand.

His cries wake up Uncle, Auntie,
and the Chans,
who are lying next to us, opposite Uncle.

"What's wrong?" they ask.

"I don't know," I say.
I move *Dee Dee*'s hand away.
I cry,
"Oh, his face has swollen up
and is almost covering up his left eye."

Uncle gets up.
He comes over to inspect *Dee Dee*'s face.
"Maybe he was bitten by a poisonous insect.
We need to find a doctor
before the poison gets into his bloodstream."

The Chans and other people are wide-awake now.
They suggest we inform the soldiers.
Some say the soldiers won't understand,
but they have heard that a Chinese herbal doctor
was on our boat.

Dee Dee is scared. He asks me,
"Am I going to die?"

I hold his hand tightly.
I try to suppress my fear,
"No, you won't die.
I am here.
I won't let you die."

But my hands are shaking.

54 | THE HERBAL DOCTOR

Uncle says to his wife,
"I am going to look for a doctor."
You keep an eye on *Dee Dee*."

Right away, I hear Uncle calling,
"Is there a doctor here?
A little boy has been bitten by a poisonous insect.
Is there a doctor here?"
He calls in Vietnamese and Cantonese
from space to space in the whole camp.

Sometime later,
a man holding a small cloth bag
comes with Uncle.
I recognize
he is the man
who wanted to donate a jar of coffee to the fishermen
while we were at sea.
(Later I heard that the jar of coffee was hiding
some melted-down gold.)

I beg, "Are you a doctor?
Please make my brother get well."

"I will try," he says.

He inspects *Dee Dee*'s face.

Now it is almost as big as a pig's face.

The swelling has completely covered up his left eye.

He is still crying in pain.

The doctor says to Uncle,

"Acupuncture may help to draw out the poison."

Uncle turns to me,

"Is it okay with you?"

I say, "Yes. Do it."

Dee Dee cries harder,

"I don't want him to do it. It will hurt. . . ."

The doctor says,

"You will only feel like someone just pinched you.

That's it."

Dee Dee still refuses until I say to him,

"You will die if the poison stays inside."

It works.

He calms down right away.

He lets the doctor clean his face

with a wet cloth

while I hold his hands
and Auntie holds his legs in case he kicks.

The doctor tells *Dee Dee* to close his eyes and relax
while he inserts the first needle into his face.
Dee Dee doesn't complain.
He lets the doctor insert more needles
into his face
and a couple on his arms and legs.

Dee Dee's face looks like a porcupine
with its quills standing out.

The doctor says *Dee Dee* is a good patient.

He lets the needles stay in *Dee Dee* for a while
before he takes them all out.

"The pain and swelling should go down
in a couple of days,"
he tells Uncle.
He must think that we are Uncle's children
until I try to give him my jade *Kwun Yum*
for payment.

He doesn't take it, but says,
"We are all in the same boat.
We should help one another out."

55 | *DEE DEE'S* CONDITION

Dee Dee sleeps for two or three hours.
The swelling on his face
is still pumped up,
but the pain has diminished.

The doctor comes back to check on him.
Dee Dee complains that he is hungry.
The doctor says
that it is a good sign.
He instructs *Dee Dee* to rest for a couple more days
and not to run around
until the swelling goes down.

I am very surprised that *Dee Dee* doesn't protest.

I tell my *ma, ah mah,* and *baba*
silently that
we really have met a noble family
and a noble doctor.

56 | THE NECESSITIES

Uncle gets his purchases.
There are four mats to enclose their own sleeping space,
a pot for cooking rice and also to serve as a teapot,
bowls that can serve as teacups,
chopsticks that can also serve as a spatula,
a wok,
a bucket with a rope, a can opener,
an ax, a few candles with matches, and
several packages of insect repellant.

He says
since nobody knows
how long they will have to stay in this camp,
and they need to save the gold for the unknown future,
he just got the basic necessities
like other people did.

My throat feels tight again
as Uncle hands me two bowls,
two pairs of chopsticks,
two candles with matches,
and a couple of packages of insect repellant
to chase the mosquitoes away.
I receive them with both hands
to show respect.

And I swear in my heart:

I will always remember you,

Uncle.

I will always remember you,

Auntie.

57 | OUR FIRST COOKED MEAL

To save firewood,
Auntie suggests that
we cook all the food together
instead of waiting for our turn to cook.

I am very thankful.
I hand her all our rice,
instant noodles,
and canned goods,
and we share food with them
like a big family.

Uncle takes his new ax,
and Nam, Dao, and I follow him
to get firewood.

Dee Dee wants to join us
so he doesn't miss the adventure.
Auntie says, "I don't think it is a good idea
for you
to move around.
You are not completely well yet."

Dee Dee doesn't protest.
He minds Auntie

better than he minded *Ma* and *Ah Mah* back home.

I really don't want to leave *Dee Dee*.
Auntie sees through me and says,
"I will keep a close eye on him while you are gone."

We find some dry palm tree fronds,
and Uncle chops some small branches with the new ax.
Each of us
drags a handful of fronds
and branches back to the camp.

Auntie has already dug two holes in the ground,
surrounded by a circle of rocks,
and she has put the wok and pot on top of them
as stoves.

Soon, smoke is rising everywhere.
Soon, the campsite is diffused with
the fragrance of rice,
instant noodles,
and the canned food cooking.

We have fresh rice
cooked with well water

instead of salty sea water.

We have curry chicken,
stirred with
canned green beans.

We drink fresh-brewed jasmine tea
while Uncle and Auntie drink black coffee.

It's by far the best meal
that we've had
since we left home!

58 | LIFE IN THE TEMPORARY CAMP

Our most urgent job is finding firewood.
Auntie cooks;
Dao and I help.

Dao and I wash dishes.

Uncle gets well water
and sips tea or coffee with friends he just made.
Sometimes he returns with green or ripe coconuts
that his friends have found or picked.
He makes sure everyone has some coconut water
and meat.
"The only vitamin C we can get right now," he says.

While many people, especially the young men,
swim every day,
we take our baths next to the well
by pouring water over ourselves
from head to toe.
We change clothes
in Uncle's "house."
But Auntie is happy just to have a sponge bath.

While Auntie and Dao wash their clothes
around the well,

I wash *Dee Dee*'s and mine.

We hang our clothes on the rope
suspended between two palm trees
or just drape them on top of the shrubs.

The colorful clothing waving in the breeze
around the whole campsite
reminds me of prayer flags
on the hills in Tibet
that I saw in my textbook back home.

59 | LEECHES

Dee Dee's face eventually goes back to normal.
He joins us to get firewood.
I am so thankful for the doctor who
didn't ask for anything in return.

Once in the woods,
Dao points behind me and says,
"You have leeches on your foot!"

I jump.

Two leeches are sucking my blood
on my bare right heel.
I cry and try to pull them off,
but Dao stops me, saying,
"Don't!"

She runs back and gets a box of matches.
She lights a match, blows it out gently, and says,
"Don't move."
I stand still while she moves the smoking match
close to where the leeches are
until they drop off my heel.

I am very grateful to Dao as I say,

"I am terrified of leeches."

"The leeches do not bother me.
I got used to them when we visited my *bà ngoại*
in the countryside.
I am only scared of snakes.
I panic if I see them."

Dao lets me wear her sandals
because I am barefoot.

I tell her sincerely,
"I will return the favor to you
whenever I have the chance."

She shakes her head
and waves her hand.
"Don't bother," she says.
"I don't expect anything
in return."

I like her.

60 | UNCLE MAKING FRIENDS

We have a lot of spare time.
Uncle and the doctor
sometimes join the old comers
as they fish in the late afternoon.

Very often
they use long, slim tree branches
as fishing poles to fish at the shore.
It isn't an easy task.

Once, they catch a tiny fish
and grill it over the fire.
Oh, the whole campsite is infused
with the aroma of roasted fish
that everybody longs for,
because we all miss eating fish,
like we did back home.

Some brave single men make a raft
with large branches lashed together
and go farther out into the sea to fish.
But some do not return.
Their raft must have been swept away,
or it must have sunk.
That's why Auntie always prays that

Uncle and his friends
will never go out to the ocean
on a raft
but will just fish at the shore.

61 | AUNTIE MAKING FRIENDS

Auntie makes friends with
the Chans who are next to our space.
They share some coconuts that
their twins, Number One and Number Two,
picked from the trees.

Auntie also makes friends with the ladies
while they are washing clothes around the well.
They compare their lives here
to their lives back home.
Some had maids to serve them,
but now they have to do everything
themselves.
They hope
that they will have a maid
to serve them
when they settle down in the new land.

And they wonder
if
their dream will come true.

62 | DAO AND I MAKING FRIENDS

Dao and I make friends
with two girls named Ming and Jan.
They are the same age as us.
We take turns jumping rope
one by one,
or
two of us jump while the other two
twirl the rope.

Sometimes we just stroll along the bay
after supper,
trying to find the best seashells
or pick up the dried driftwood
as fuel
and look at the beautiful sunset.

Or sometimes we just whisper jokes
and cover our mouths,
giggling.

We even go to the latrine
together.
It is safer than just Dao and me going.

63 | *DEE DEE*, NAM, AND THEIR NEW FRIENDS

Uncle ties two ropes
between two tall palm trees
as a swing for Nam and *Dee Dee*.
One rope is higher,
for the back to lean on,
and one rope is lower,
to sit on.
It attracts many kids.
They are so noisy
and sometimes argue,
"Me first!"

And when someone falls
from the swing,
they laugh their heads off,
like they are not in the camp
but on the school playground back home.

Sometimes *Dee Dee* and Nam,
along with their friends,
all naked from the waist up,
wade into the shallow water
of the small bay
or race as the waves crash on the shore.

Then they all line up and
dry themselves on the sand,
like people back home
hanging fish on a clothesline
to dry.

In reality,

I do not like strolling at the bay.

I do not like seeing the ocean.

It makes me feel like I am

being rocked up and down by the huge waves.

There are about ten refugee boats

anchored in the bay not far from shore.

I don't want to see them again.

I hope that

I won't sail on that kind of boat ever again.

Dao says she doesn't like the sun, either.

It will darken her skin.

She and Auntie have the kind of fair skin

that most girls wish for.

So we stay in the shade, where

the view of all the boats is blocked,

while Jan and Ming look for seashells.

Dao and I share our dreams.

I tell her

I hope *Dee Dee* and I will live in San Francisco

with my *baba,*

and we will ask him to take us

to Disneyland

and to see real snow.

"Oh!" Dao cries,
"I want to meet Snow White.
I want to see real snow, too.
How come we are thinking
the same thing?"

I suggest,
"When we are in America,
you can visit us in San Francisco,
and we can go to Disneyland together.
In the winter,
we can all go to see and feel the snow!"

She cries,
"How nice!
Do you know what?
I haven't known you very long,
but I like you.
I don't get along very well with my brother.
I wish you were my sister."

I say,
"I didn't get along with my brother, either.

We always fought back home,
and my *ma* often scolded me.
But now, *Dee Dee* is my everything,
and I am his everything."

We declare
we will go to Disneyland together
to see Snow White;
and we will see snow
and touch snow in the winter
together.

And I also find out that
Uncle's mother is Chinese.
I feel even
closer to Dao
and her family.

65 | THE BAD NEWS AND GOOD NEWS

Like fire burning,
bad and sad news spreads fast
throughout the whole camp.

A baby dies.
I don't know why.
One man donates a mat to wrap the body in
and helps bury it farther away from the campsite.
The mother can't bring herself
to see her little baby
being put into the ground.

The happy times are
seeing the Red Cross workers come.
They distribute the food
and take the sick away
for treatment.

And everybody looks forward to
being sent to a regular camp
to be interviewed.

That day is
worth waiting for.

66 | UNCLE'S PLAN

I have lost track
of how many days we have been here.
Some say about two weeks.
Some say it seems longer.
It doesn't matter
as long as we are with Uncle and Auntie.

One day, Uncle, a former high school math teacher,
says that he doesn't know
how long it will be
before we can go to a regular camp.
He decides to teach Nam and Dao math
and English after breakfast
and postpones their chores
until the afternoon.

He asks *Dee Dee* and me
if we would like to join them.
He says his English is limited,
but he will teach us as much as he can.

I say okay.

Dee Dee is reluctant.
He wants to play with Nam.

But Nam has lessons, too.
Dee Dee says he will do
whatever Nam is going to do.

Auntie clears up the space
between her "house"
and our "house without walls"
for our classroom.

Uncle uses the sandy ground
as the blackboard
and a stick
as chalk.
We sit in a semicircle around him.
Very often,
we have to stand up to get a better look
at what he has written in the sand.

Nam and Dao's English is the best.
They learned some
before they left Vietnam.

Dee Dee and I don't have a clue,
but we repeat what Uncle says.
"Hello, my name is Lam Chan. I am Chinese," I say.
"Hello, my name is Yan Chan. I am Chinese," *Dee Dee* says.

Dee Dee and I giggle.

It is the first time we hear our names
in English.
Uncle tells us to remember it.
But when the lesson is over,
I can't remember
even a single word.

68 | TO UNCLE'S SURPRISE

To Uncle's surprise,
on the second day after we start our lessons,
Ming and Jan and their brothers want to join.
They bring a piece of board with them
for the blackboard.

Uncle hangs the board on a palm tree next to us.
Auntie gives him the half-burned twigs
that have turned into charcoal from cooking
to use as chalk.
We don't need to stand up to look
at what Uncle has written
as he guides Dao and me
in how to solve a word problem.

Uncle uses one of his shirts as an eraser.
It is very messy.
Charcoal often soils his hands all over.
But I have not heard him complain.

By word of mouth, by the fifth day,
there are a total of ten students.
This is very surprising to Uncle.
Some parents even buy chalk for him to use
while teaching.

Uncle is ecstatic
about having a board and chalk for teaching.
After that, he often forgets about the time
and just keeps talking.
Now he doesn't have as much time to sip tea
with his friends as before
because he is busy preparing his lessons
on the board.

69 | THE FIREWOOD

The dry firewood
is getting harder and harder to find.
There are some male teens
who will get firewood for the elderly
or for the rich
in exchange for cooking utensils
or what they need.
That's why
we have to chop the green twigs
and let them dry in the sun for days
before they can be burned.

That's why
we often hear arguments
as someone accuses another of
stealing their firewood.

After he teaches us for about one week,
Uncle's friends convince him to take a break
and go fishing with them on a raft.

Auntie objects strongly.
Uncle is reluctant,
for he is the one who often chops firewood,
and he needs to prepare
for his English lesson
and make up math problems for
different levels.

He finally agrees to go
out of curiosity.
He convinces Auntie that
they won't be unlucky.
So he instructs us
to just collect the dry wood
without the ax
and reminds us
to stay in a group
and beware of snakes.

71 | DAO'S SECRET

We four—myself, Dao, *Dee Dee,* and Nam—
go out to the woods.
Without Uncle around,
Dee Dee and Nam are like two wild monkeys.
They run in the woods with their other friends.
They play tag, chasing and laughing
all the way.

In the woods,
Dao looks into the distance and says,
"Oh, the twins are there ahead of us."

I say, "I am glad. I like more people
in the woods."
She whispers, eyeing them, "Who is cuter?
Twin Number One or Twin Number Two?"

I am shocked.
I have never thought about them.
I have never talked with them
because
they are boys.

"I like Twin Number One more," says Dao.
"I like the tiny mole on his right cheek."

I am even more shocked.
How could she observe them so
carefully?

Her eyes are following the twins
as she is saying, like in a dream,
"I hope I can see him
in America.
But . . .
this is a secret.
I have told only you."

And I promise her
that I will never tell anyone.
I am very fortunate that
Dao has shared her secret with me.

Only me.

72 | A SUDDEN STRIKE

The twins disappear into the dense woods.
Dao is still dreaming,
still searching
for her secret crush
until she lets out a sharp cry
in front of a thick bush.

"What happened?" I ask, suddenly alert.

"Something has bitten me!
A snake . . .
Help me!"

"Where?"

"My right foot!" She hops on her left foot
while she lifts the other foot up from the ground.

I am in a panic, but I try to see her wound
and yell at the same time,
"Help! Dao got bit by a snake! Help!"

The kids rush toward us.
The twins run toward us.
"What kind of snake?" they ask.

"I don't know. It was brown.
It retreated back into the bushes."

"It may have been a cobra,"
Twin Number One says as he takes off his shirt.
"Where did it bite you?"

"On my right ankle."

I shiver and order the kids,
"Go get the doctor!"

Nam is trembling.
He can't say a word.

Dee Dee reminds me,
"The doctor and Uncle have gone fishing."

"Go get a soldier!" Twin Number One commands,
ready to tie a tourniquet above Dao's ankle
with his shirt,
while Twin Number Two drops on his knees
to find the puncture wound.

"We don't know how to say it," *Dee Dee* says.

"Use your hands!" Twin Number One orders.

Dee Dee and Nam run off to inform the soldiers,
while Dao cries,
"It burns. It feels like my foot is on fire!"
She doesn't let them touch her foot,
which appears
black
and blue
and purple
and swells to almost twice its normal size.

"I have to suck the poison out," Twin Number Two yells
as he grabs her foot.
Dao struggles and cries, "No, no."
She kicks.

Twin Number One can't tie on the tourniquet, either.

"You will die if you don't let them!" I cry.

We use force.
I hold on to her.

One twin holds her foot.
The other twin finally ties the tourniquet
above her ankle.
Dao struggles.
Dao kicks as the twin tries to suck the poison out.
She cries, "Someone is stabbing my chest
with a knife. . . ."

She is about to escape my grip.
I have a hard time holding her.
She is gasping for air.
"I . . . I can't breathe. . . .
A rock is on . . . my chest. . . ."
I think
I hear Dao's heartbeats,
like they are pounding
out of her chest.

"Let me carry her back, quick!" Twin Number One
suggests.
"I am afraid the poison will get to her heart!"
Twin Number Two and I manage to put Dao
on his back.

Twin Number One begins to run.

We run next to them

and help Dao stay on his back.

But Dao slumps to one side

and is about to fall.

She has passed out.

73 | DAO

Many people from the campsite
run toward us.
A soldier is ahead of them.
He stops Twin Number One and helps Dao down.
Dao is motionless.
He checks on her and opens her eyelids.

He says something.

We don't understand
until he shakes his head without saying
a word.

I have no fear of the gun
he carries on his shoulder.

"Dao, Dao!"
Auntie holds on to Dao,
crying and saying,
"You will be okay.
Your *cha* will be here;
the doctor will be here;
you will be okay. . . ."

Dao doesn't respond.

She is dead.

Auntie is wailing.
Nam and *Dee Dee* are crying.
Other people shake their heads
as the twins walk away,
heads down.

I stand away from the crowd
without tears.
I can't believe that
Dao is gone.
It can't be real.
She just told me her secret
a short while ago.

I don't move until
the soldier
carries Dao back to the camp.
I support Auntie
and follow them.

74 | I AM MAD AT MYSELF

Uncle is full of regret and feels guilty
for going fishing.
He believes that if he had been near,
Dao's life could have been saved.

Auntie blames him
for their daughter's death.
She sits next to Dao's body,
next to their "house,"
wailing and calling Dao's name.
It makes many other people shed tears.

I am afraid to look at Dao.
I am mad at myself.
She helped me get rid of the leeches,
but I couldn't help her get rid of the poison.

I am also mad at Dao.
If she had let the twins
suck the poison out
or tie the shirt above the bite earlier
instead of struggling,
she might not be gone.

I am mad at everybody!

That day

Mrs. Chan sends food to us.

I thank her.

But no one eats.

No one feels hungry,

not even *Dee Dee*.

75 | NOTHING COMES OUT

The next day
there are no lessons.

The doctor delivers a few boards
that he has collected from his friends.
Our captain,
whose head wound has healed,
comes with two sailors.
They make a simple coffin with the boards
for Dao.

Auntie won't let go of Dao's body
as Uncle,
whose face is streaked with tears,
tries to place Dao into the coffin.

Auntie wishes she was with her daughter.
Uncle pleads with her.
He promises Auntie that
after they have settled down,
they will return to transfer Dao's body
to where they are.

Still,
Auntie refuses to watch Dao being buried.

Mrs. Chan stays behind with her.

The soldier who carried Dao before
helps Uncle find a place for her
on a small hill nearby.

Not many people come:
only the doctor,
the twins,
the captain,
and a few others.

I can't watch Dao being buried.
I still can't believe that
Dao is gone.

We planned to see each other
again in America.
We planned to see Snow White
and feel the snow
together.

After the burial,
I do not leave right away.
I want to tell Dao

many,
many things,
but
nothing comes out.

76 | THE GRIEF

Auntie sleeps all day inside the mat house.
Uncle smokes quietly next to it.
It is the first time I have seen him smoke.
Nam doesn't want to play and
stays with his *ma*.
Dee Dee and I take up the household chores:
boiling the water
for coffee and tea,
cooking,
and washing.

If Dao could be alive again,
I wouldn't mind doing all the chores
day after day.
But Uncle tells me
after we burn all our firewood,
we will just eat the food
right from the cans.
He doesn't want us going into the woods
again.

Auntie has not had a bite of food
since Dao died.
Nam and Uncle eat just a little.
I don't have any appetite

as I notice the extra chopsticks and bowl
for Dao.

77 | THREE GROUPS

A couple days after Dao's passing,
a translator reads off the names
of people in our boat.

They divide us into three groups.
The doctor, the old couple whose niece died,
Dee Dee, and I are in the first group.
The Chan family and Ming and Jan
are in the second group.
Uncle and his family
and all the Vietnamese and single males
are in the third group.

The translator doesn't give us any details.
People are murmuring among themselves, smiling.
They assume that all three groups will be sent
to different refugee camps.

They are content,
for they are finally going to the regular camps:
to get to interview,
to get on the waiting list,
to get to the new land.

The old lady in black kneels down and gives thanks.

She declares with joy,
"How lucky we are!
We have stayed in this camp
for less than a month,
and now we are going to a regular camp!"

More old ladies give thanks,
while the old comers
envy and wonder
in silence.

I am not sure.
I am happy and sad at the same time.
A knot is inside my heart.
What about Dao?
What if we are separated from Uncle and Auntie?

The translator announces that
the third group will be leaving first
to go to another place within the hour.
Everyone in the third group should pack
immediately.
The first and second groups will follow.

We are dismissed

to pack our belongings.

I am disheartened at this announcement.

I follow Uncle back to our "houses."

He stops and waits for us.

He whispers,

"You and *Dee Dee* come with us,

but don't say anything

and don't ask any questions.

Just keep it between us."

My eyes cloud with tears.

He is mourning his daughter,

but he is still thinking about us.

I am even more touched by his

kindness.

I am no longer worried that

Dee Dee and I will be separated

from them.

Dee Dee is overjoyed.

"Are we going to America now?"

"Not yet," Uncle replies.

Dee Dee and I do not have much to pack.
I help Uncle pack the pot,
bowls,
and mats.
Auntie, who didn't go for the announcement,
is still crying
and sometimes just stares into space.

She hasn't eaten for days;
she just sips tea.
I want to comfort her.
But I don't know what to say.

We all take a brisk walk to say goodbye to Dao,
all except for Auntie.

Dao is resting underneath the biggest tree,
where Uncle wrote Dao's name on a piece of board
on top of the newly piled up dirt
as a grave marker.

I say to Dao quietly,
"Goodbye, Dao.
I promise I will go to Disneyland
to see Snow White for you.

I promise I will touch and feel the snow
for you.
I promise I will keep your secret
for you.
I promise I will try my best to help care for your *ma,*
your *baba,* and Nam.
You rest and don't worry."

Dao doesn't say a word.
Dao doesn't answer me.

79 | WAITING

The third group is ready to leave.
Dee Dee holds the plastic sheets.
I hold the bucket
with bowls and canned food inside.
Uncle takes the pot and the mats.
Nam holds his mother's hand and supports her
since she doesn't want Uncle to touch her.

We quietly stand next to Uncle.
We wait
to board the buses
that are parked next to the soldiers' shed.

The mother whose baby died
at the camp
doesn't want to leave.
Her husband tries to convince her
to go, and he weeps
so brokenheartedly
it seems
as if all the trees around us
shed tears for them.

I spot Twin Number One.
I feel like something is squeezing my heart.

If not for him,
could Dao still be alive?
Or was it just her bad fate?
And should I tell him
that such a beautiful girl
had a crush on him?

But I decide
I already promised Dao that
the secret
belongs only to
Dao
and me.

80 | BOARDING THE BUS

There are soldiers guarding the buses.

The translator calls out names.
Whenever he calls a person's name,
they will board the bus
along with their belongings.

I am frightened,
even when
Uncle whispers to *Dee Dee* and me,
"Don't say anything
and don't ask any questions.
We will be on the same bus."

I want so badly
to ask Uncle
How?
My mind is unsettled,
like something is hanging
in my heart.

Uncle's name is called.
He approaches the bus
but doesn't board it.
Instead he says, "I am waiting for my family."

The translator announces,
"The Nguyen family members!"

Auntie has stopped crying,
but she seems glued to the ground,
despite how much Nam urges her.
Uncle scolds us loudly,
"Didn't you hear?
Are you still angry with one another?
Help your mother!
Move!"

I get it.
He wants me to take Dao's place.
What about *Dee Dee*?
I shoot a questioning glance at Uncle.
I don't want to leave *Dee Dee*
behind.

Uncle continues to ignore me,
demanding,
"Come quick! Don't make other people wait!"

I remember how he told me earlier,
"Don't say anything,

and don't ask any questions."
Immediately,
I hold Auntie's other side
while Nam helps her on his side.
I look over my shoulder
and motion
for *Dee Dee* to follow us.

I am very thankful that
Auntie is cooperative
and willing to move.

Together
we approach the bus,
but my heart is thumping
like a tap dancer.
I am afraid the soldier
who carried Dao is there.
I am afraid the interpreter
will look at the list
and find out the truth.
I am afraid that someone in the camp
will blurt out that
I am not their daughter.

But my worry
turns out to be nothing.
We reach the bus,
even though my hands are still
shaking.

And I feel my stomach
churning like the open sea
when I find out that
Dee Dee is still
standing in the same place,
unmoving.

I look at Uncle with fright.
He again ignores me
but hastily
stomps over to where *Dee Dee* is
and slaps him in the face,
hard.

Dee Dee bursts out crying.

Uncle drags him by his arm,
scolding,
"Why are you still throwing temper tantrums?"
He hoists him up onto the bus
and pushes him down into a seat,
hard.

I understand
and let out a silent sigh of relief.
I help Auntie board the bus
and squeeze into a seat opposite Uncle,
without saying a word.
I notice Uncle is trying to
control his hands
from shaking.

There are two soldiers with guns
sitting behind us.
As if a clock is in my heart,
I am counting each second,
hoping the bus will take off immediately
before the soldiers
discover the truth.

So I sit like a statue
too nervous
to turn my head aside
to say thanks to the people
who are wishing us good luck.

I just close my eyes and tell myself,
Be calm.
The soldier behind us will sense that
I am tense
until the engine of the bus
comes to life
and we set off.

I give a "thank you" nod to Uncle
and he returns it with a
nod of assurance.

We get off next to a small ferry
where an old refugee boat is docked.

We are told to get into the boat
after the soldiers distribute a bag of food
to everyone.
Some are suspicious, asking,
"Why are we going back to a boat?
Aren't they supposed to take us
to the regular camp?"

Someone says,
"They never told us where they were taking us.
We just assumed that we are going to the camp."

It is true.
We quiet down.

Uncle asks one of the soldiers.
The soldier simply says,
"Just get into the boat."

"I am sick of riding boats again!"
I complain and so do the others.

We have no choice
but to do what we are told.
We are just like a kite in the sky that
is controlled by its kite flyer.

We are facing
the unknown.

PART THREE

June 11, 1979
South China Sea

83 | TOWARD THE OPEN SEA

A big ship is anchored at a distance
from the shore.
Two other refugee boats are floating
behind it in a row,
between our boat and the big ship.

After we all board the boat,
the big ship begins to move.

Soon the first refugee boat that is
closest to the big ship sails.
The other boat behind it
moves ahead.
Then our boat,
slowly following the second one,
leaves the dock
with nobody on board piloting it.

It is then that we discover
the big ship is towing all three refugee boats,
one after another,
like a long train.
Our boat is the caboose.

We are perplexed.

So is the captain.
Why is the big ship towing us?

Some guess,
"It might save a lot of gas
while towing us to the refugee camp."
Others agree.
Someone says, "It is still too early to say."

After being towed
for two days and two nights nonstop,
it seems the refugee camp is
on the other side of the world.

People start asking questions
about this endless towing.
"Where is the camp?
We could have gone halfway
around the world by now!"

Others try to comfort them, declaring,
"You don't need to worry about where we are
as long as they are towing us,
as long as they are with us."

Most of the people agree
and go back to sleep.

I feel so sick
I can't sleep,
like many other people,
as our boat is being thrown
up and down.

And suddenly we hear
a loud sound.
It sounds close.
It sounds different from the time
the fishermen cut our rope.

Everyone is suddenly awake,
wondering
where the sound has come from.
Someone shines a flashlight
around
to check.

We don't see anything.
We try to go back to sleep,
but then someone screams,
"Water!
Water is coming into the boat!"
More flashlights shoot toward
where the noise is coming from.
People are rushing toward
the source of the noise.

The captain goes to investigate
and soon returns, declaring,
"The front of the boat has split!
The dragon bone has broken
because they have been towing
this old boat from the front.
We need strong men
to help bail the water out

before it sinks!"

Uncle and some men go up
with the captain right away.

The men form a bucket brigade immediately.
They take buckets
and go down a hatch in the front of the boat.
Soon they send the buckets of water
up
and the men on the deck
dump it,
then return
the empty buckets to those down below.

They repeat this task
nonstop.

Meanwhile, people
yell in the darkness in
Cantonese, Mandarin, and Vietnamese,
"Giúp tôi! Giúp tôi!"
"Help! Our boat is sinking!"

Some shine flashlights to get the attention

of the big ship,
but the lights are swallowed up
by the darkness.
The yelling is ripped away
by the roaring wind.

But they keep yelling!
They keep shining the flashlights.
They keep bailing out the water.

85 | THE NIGHTMARE

The second boat, the one in front of us,
hears us.
They yell for us.
The first one hears them.
They yell for us.
But the big ship does not hear them.
It keeps sailing on.
Strangely, it sails
farther and farther away,
completely immersed in the darkness.

The soldiers do not hear us.

It is then that
our captain notices that
our boat is just drifting,
although we are still tied to the
second boat.
The soldiers must have cut the towrope
to the first boat
without any warning.
When?
Before the dragon bone broke?
No one knows,
not even the captain.

So all three of our refugee boats
are just drifting
in the dark open ocean.

86 | INSIDE THE CABIN

The fury of our anger
over being betrayed again explodes
like dragon's fire
bursting up to the sky,
as our captain discovers that
the engine in our boat
doesn't work.

Someone declares,
"Maybe they messed up the boat on purpose
so we can't get back to land!"

Some agree;
some are not sure.
One says calmly,
"I am not sure about that.
Maybe it was disabled by other refugees before,
like how we sabotaged ours."

"Oh, yes," we remember.
The angry voices
die down.

Just then the sailor with rotten teeth reports,
"There are two full barrels of water

and a bag of rice
in the storage room."

This ignites a flame of anger
once more.
Someone says,
"That's why they left us the water and rice!
They know they are guilty!"

Another declares,
"We should be glad that
they still have a conscience
to leave us water and rice."

The old man in blue cries out,
"Having a conscience or no conscience,
we still face the same fate!"

The old lady in black
wails,
"How pitiful we are!
Buddha hasn't blessed us!
We will all be drowned for sure."

Someone shouts,

"Shut up! You're getting on my nerves!"

But the old lady in black
doesn't shut up;
she keeps on wailing,
"There's no use in having water and rice.
We are all going to drown!"

Babies and small children seem to know
what is ahead of us
and cry with fear,
no matter how much
their mothers try to comfort them.

Dee Dee holds me tightly and asks,
"Are we going to die?"

I can't answer him.

The whole boat is facing
a disaster.

Auntie appears to be
the calmest of all.
She doesn't cry,

she doesn't ask,
she doesn't say a word,
as if the world is far
beyond her.

Seeing that,
I am scared and sad
at the same time.

87 | DRIFTING

Three boats are drifting in the vast sea,
surrounded by the darkness.
All three boats,
which are not our original boats,
have the same fate:
their engines don't work.

Without knowing the direction we are drifting,
without knowing where we are,
without knowing if a storm will come
at any minute,
we are all in danger of being
swallowed up by the open sea.

The captains and sailors
are helpless.
They just let the boats drift. . . .

88 | WE SEE LIGHT

Dawn comes on the third day.
The first boat,
whose engine apparently had only minor damage,
has sailed away.

Our boat and the second one
remain adrift at sea.

Our captain makes a deal with the second boat,
that both captains will help each other
to repair the engines.

We see light at the end of the tunnel.

Our people pull the other boat
close to ours.
Our captain jumps over to the other boat,
to help repair their engine
as both captains have promised.

By noon, their boat is fixed.
People in the other boat
cheer.

Our spirits lift

as the other boat's captain
comes to help fix our engine.
Several old people declare that
Buddha, the Heaven God, *Duc Me*, and *Kwun Yum*
haven't left us.
They are still blessing us.

The two captains don't stop working
as two groups of strong men, taking turns,
continue bailing out the water
nonstop.

In the evening, we hear the engine come to life.
All faces light up with hope
and people cheer,
"We can navigate now!"
But the engine sputters a few times
and dies.

"The engine can't be fixed
without a replacement part,"
both captains announce.

There is silence,
like that of the dead.

89 | TOWING AGAIN

Our captain negotiates with the other captain.
They agree to tow us
without getting anything in return.
We are very thankful to their kind captain.

They tie two ropes, one on each side of our boat,
and begin to tow us.
But our boat is heavy,
and the water keeps coming in,
despite how hard the men bail it out
constantly.

On the fourth day,
we see a shadow far away.
It looks like we are close to land,
but, with regret, the other captain unties our boat.
They fear that they are going to run out of gas
from towing our heavy boat.
They say we are close to the shore,
and they will send someone to help us.
Then the boat motors away.

Our people are furious
and curse,
all except Auntie.

They ask,
"How can they find someone to help?
It is just an excuse to get rid of us!"

"They don't honor their words.
They will all die in a hard way!"

"They are ungrateful!"

It is the captain who tries to cool
the boiling water down.
He says,
"Stop cursing and yelling.
It won't help a bit.
I understand your concern.
But we can't just let our boat drift.
We have avoided being attacked by pirates.
We have to find a way to let our boat make progress."

"How?" several people ask.

"We haven't figured that out yet," he declares.

Some young men suggest,
"Let's abandon the boat

and swim toward the shore!"

The older people reject that idea
and claim,
"No! We will drown for sure!"

The captain says to the young men,
"Swimming toward the shore
is not a wise solution.
It is much farther than you may think."

"So, let the boat just drift?"

"No. We won't let our boat just drift,"
the captain replies.

90 | THEIR SPIRITS ARE HIGH

Someone is breaking up
something on top of us.
Dee Dee goes to have a look.
"They are trying to get boards off the deck!"
he reports.

"Why?" people ask.

"I don't know."

Soon
there are about eight people
who were waiting for their turn
to bail out the water
paddling the boat
with the long boards
that they took from the deck.

They paddle in the direction of the shadow
that's now far away.

Our boat is moving slowly forward.
People are smiling.
They praise the captain
and his crew members.

More men come up to join in,
giving the paddlers a hand.

Their spirits are high.
Together they bail, with the rhythm of the water bailing;
they paddle, with the rhythm of the paddling,
they chant, with the rhythm of their breathing,
despite their dripping sweat
mingling with the spray of the breaking waves.

When one group takes a rest,
another group comes up
without any interruption.
They continue to strike
toward the land,
toward victory.

91 | RELAXED

People in the cabin are more relaxed than ever.
They continue to eat their own food
and get water from the barrel.

Despite my seasickness,
I stumble to the storage room.
I use our pot to scoop out water.
But the water is being depleted quickly.
Compared to the last time I got the water,
there is less than half a barrel in both barrels.
Yet the rice is untouched.

I gently shake Auntie and implore her to eat
while Nam and *Dee Dee* are eating their food.
She refuses.
I beg, "Please, Auntie."

Nam cries and threatens,
"If you don't eat,
I won't, either."

It works.
Auntie and I eat together.
She eats one piece of cracker and
sips some water.

I am happy.
Nam is happier.

I grope my way onto the deck
with the water and food.
Uncle has been bailing out the water
and is now waiting for his turn to paddle.
He is so glad to see me.
He asks if Auntie is eating anything.
I tell him the truth.
"Good," he says
and lets out a long sigh.

Strong winds rise
as dusk falls.

One paddler cries,
"Captain! We seem to have lost our direction.
It seems we are in the middle of nowhere!"

All the paddlers stop paddling,
as if they agree.
The shadow is no longer in sight!
The troop is defeated by unseen enemies.
They debate.
Some say one direction,
and others say the opposite.
Even the captain
is hard-pressed to say where they should head.

Our boat is surrounded by
water, wind, waves, and darkness.
We are alone.
We can't distinguish where the edge of the sky is
from the edge of the water.
They look like they are
merged.

Our boat really is
in the middle of nowhere.

93 | THE BROKEN COMPASS

The captain orders,
"NO
ONE
TURN
ON
A
FLASHLIGHT."

He fears they might attract pirates.

The paddlers all come back down
to the cabin,
so discouraged that they don't want to talk.
They only want to sleep.
And the strong men
who are bailing out the water
are getting slower and slower
in their task.

The old man in blue complains,
"Why didn't they look at the compass?"

An angry paddler fights back.
"Shut up! It was broken long ago!
Why don't you just move your butt

and paddle yourself!"

The old man in blue keeps quiet.

Dee Dee asks me,
"What are we going to do now?"

"Don't ask me!" I snap.
My mood is as bad as the paddler
who told the old man in blue to shut up.

94 | THE OLD LADY IN BLACK

The old lady in black cries all night long.
"We are waiting to die!
We are being punished
because of our sins. . . ."

No one shouts at her.
I wish I could stick a cloth in her mouth
and shut her up.

She keeps ranting and runs up to the deck,
screaming,
"The Heaven God has punished all of us!
I am going to ask the Heaven God for mercy!"

Her daughter and son pull her back.
She grows much stronger.
They are unable to stop her,
until a couple of men hold her down.

For her safety,
they lock her in the storage room
after removing the water and rice.

We still hear her chilling cries.

95 | AUNTIE

With so much going on
and the screaming of the old lady in black,
Auntie, still lying there,
has not once opened her eyes
to investigate.
It's as if she is in another world.

Her body shrinks smaller each day.
I fear that someday
she will just melt away.
I can't believe that
she is the same gentle auntie
who cared for us
before.

I squeeze her bony hand for a second.
I do not know what to say.
I squeeze Nam's hand.
He has been sitting next to his *ma*
the whole time.
I do not know what to say to him,
either.

96 | UNCLE'S WORDS

Uncle comes back to the cabin in despair.
He says to me,
"I should not have asked you
to come with us.
You might have already settled down."
He sighs.
"I did it with good intentions,
but I am sorry
it has turned out like this."

I express myself from the bottom of my heart,
"I am so thankful to you for taking us.
You and Auntie are like parents to us.
We will stay with you
no matter what,
without any regrets."

"I appreciate you trusting us.
I hope everything
will turn out good," he says.

"I know it will.
When the sun comes up tomorrow,
boats will spot us."

"I hope you are right," Uncle says.
He is exhausted,
but fears it will irritate Auntie
if he lies down beside us.
He finds a space away from her
and sleeps.

97 | A SMALL LEAF

We are alone.
We see no other boats—
no refugee boats,
no pirate boats—
all day long!

We just let our boat drift by itself
as if in circles through the open sea,
since we can't determine
which direction we should go.

So
our boat is like a small leaf
floating in the huge South China Sea
without an anchor to settle it down,
without any guiding light to show it
where to sail,
with only the strong wind
that comes with the darkness.
It lifts our boat high and low,
like our cat playing with a helpless mouse
back home.

We scream.

At any minute,
our boat could be swallowed up and sink.
That is
what everybody
knows.
That is
what everybody
fears.

98 | ON THE FIFTH DAY AT SEA

On the afternoon of the fifth day,
the drinking water is gone.
The cabin is quiet,
as quiet as the dead,
except for the lady in black who
once in a while will wail
like a funeral dirge.

Some hours later, in the evening,
we hear voices yell for help on the deck.

Many people rush onto the deck.
Dee Dee, Nam, and I join, too.
The mist is very thick,
like a steam room that I once saw in a movie.
But the captain and two other sailors
are vigorously waving boards
wrapped with burning clothes above their heads.

A ship is half hiding, half appearing in the mist.
Still, we can see her white flag
with a big red rising sun
flapping against the wind.

"We will be saved at last!"

we all say, laughing,
despite the strong wind
ripping through us,
as if sending us
into the sea.

More men
take off their shirts,
smear them with engine oil,
and light them as a torch
to attract the Japanese ship.

The deck is so loud with yelling in
Mandarin, Cantonese, Vietnamese, and English.
Someone warns,
"Our boat is going to capsize.
Get the small children back to the cabin!
The boat is about to sink!"

Dee Dee, Nam, and the other small children
do not listen.
They are jumping up and yelling,
letting their energy out,
despite the wind that threatens
to knock them down.

But
the wind has swallowed our yelling;
the mist has obscured our excitement;
the waves have blocked our jumping
and even our boat,
for the Japanese ship is getting smaller and smaller.
At last, it turns into a dot
and disappears over the horizon.

Some curse,
some cry,
some scream,
some express regret.
Only Auntie
sleeps through the whole ordeal,
as if she would not wake up
even if the sky were falling down.

99 | *DEE DEE*'S QUESTION

Dee Dee asks,
with his lips cracked with blood
like a red caterpillar
clawing at his small face,
"Why didn't the boat come to save us?
Why did they turn away?
Didn't they see us?"

"They might not have seen us,
or they didn't want to be bothered," Uncle says.

"Why? Are they bad guys?"

"No. They might have felt
it was too much trouble for them,"
Uncle says.
"Don't worry. Sooner or later,
someone will rescue us."

100 | ON THE MORNING OF THE SIXTH DAY

On the morning of the sixth day,
again there is a commotion
on the deck.

Fluffy white clouds dot the blue sky.
Far away, the surface of the water looks as if
it is embroidered with brilliant stars.
We can easily see a ship
with the Republic of China, Taiwan,
written in Chinese and English.

Our captain estimates that
it is even closer to us
than the Japanese ship had been,
and they can spot us.

A spark of hope spreads to the
single Chinese men
like a forest fire.
They raise their torches and yell
in Mandarin and Cantonese,
"Chinese! We are Chinese!"

"Chinese help Chinese!"

I am weak.
I still yell,
"I'm Chinese! Chinese help Chinese!"

Dee Dee jumps up and down and yells, too.

Someone's torch burns out,
so another man raises one up.
We wait; we jump; we yell
and wait.

Again,
the ship gets smaller and smaller
after the flame of hope
has spread for about an hour,
and then dies down.

The whole cabin full of people
cry.
Some say they should not have come.
Some say they should have
died in their homeland
rather than be eaten by sea creatures. . . .
Some Vietnamese curse,
"The heartless Chinese . . .

they won't even help their own people!
They will die in a hard way!"

For the first time in my life,
I am ashamed to admit that
I am Chinese.

101 | THE BURDEN

I feel so low.
It just dawned on me that
we are a burden for others.
We are not welcome.
Our lives seem so worthless
that no one in the world
can be bothered
to give us a hand.

I want to go home.
My family would
never,
never
think
I was a burden
to them.

Dee Dee is scared.
I can see only his eyes
on his whole face.
He asks,
"Are we going to die this time?"

"Yes!" the man in blue cuts in.
"We are all waiting to die!"

It makes me mad.
I snap, "*You* die!
We are not going to die!"

Dee Dee cries.

Uncle forces a bitter smile
as he looks at me,
"I hope you are right."

I feel like crying.
It is not the uncle I have known
before this morning,
before the Taiwan ship turned us down.

I fear he will become like his wife—

losing all hope,

losing his struggle for survival.

I feel I have lost my *baba*.

I am beaten.

103 | AT DUSK ON THE SIXTH DAY

At dust on the sixth day
not many people are complaining.
Everybody knows,
even the small children, what will happen
eventually.

The paddlers have completely stopped paddling.
The men who have been taking turns
bailing out water
are exhausted
and not many people
have come to give them a hand.

There is a rumor
that the men can't keep up with the water
that is still coming in,
for the front of the boat is tilting down
even steeper.
The boat will eventually sink,
even without the rising waves.

Dee Dee complains,
"I am very hungry."

The old man in blue laughs.

"What's the difference
if you die of hunger
or with a full stomach?"

I don't feel like fighting with him.
I just hold on to *Dee Dee*'s hands.

That day,
a middle-aged man goes crazy.
He wails one second
and laughs the next.
No one tells him to shut up.

A baby dies.
The mother sobs without tears.
But no one forces the mother
to throw the baby into the water.
No one complains that
the dead body will contaminate the air.
Everybody knows,
sooner or later,
that he or she will become like the baby.

The captain apologizes to us sadly
for this outcome.

He says our fate is in other people's hands
and that he is still hoping
for the best.

No one says a word.

Yes. I agree.
Our fate *is* in other people's hands.
I believe that
not everybody is as heartless as the captains of
the Japanese and Taiwanese ships.
Like Uncle has said,
not every soldier is
as mean as the one who beat up our captain.

So I believe
if there is a ship out there,
there can still be
hope!

But right now,
I can't look to see if a ship is coming.
I don't want to talk;
I just want to sleep,
like Auntie,
like the rest of the people in the cabin.

So I fall into a deep, deep sleep and dream.
One second I am high, high up
in the sky;
the next second I am down, down

to the bottom of the valley.
Then I am being thrown up to the sky
again. . . .

Someone shakes me.
It is *Dee Dee*.
He cries, "They have spotted a Russian ship!"

No one moves;
no one gets up to have a look.
There is very little disturbance.

Uncle lets out a laugh.
"Huh, a Russian ship!"

Some others sneer.
They say, "The Japanese and Taiwanese ships
didn't help us.
Do you think a Communist Russian ship will?"

They all agree.
Except for me!

I try to get up
and almost faint.

I say to *Dee Dee,*
"Help me!"
I hold on to him and
together,
we drag ourselves up the steps,
up to the deck.

105 | THE RUSSIAN SHIP

It is very bright and very calm.
Is it the next day already?

Of about one hundred people,
there are only the captain
and a sailor waving their torches.
While some of the strong men
keep bailing water,
some stop;
some watch;
some wait.

I try to jump up and yell, but
I see darkness in front of me and
almost fall.
I hold on to a pole next to me and say,
"You cry for help!"

Dee Dee takes off his shirt.
He jumps;
he yells;
he waves his shirt up in the air.

"I can see the ship much more clearly!"
Dee Dee reports.

"They must have seen my shirt!"

I cry, "Yes! They are coming for us!
The Russian ship is coming for us!"

The captain and the sailor tear up.
The strong men
who are bailing out the water
are weeping.

We are not a burden.
We are welcomed;
we are worth something
to someone else in the world.
They will give us a hand
because we are
human beings!

We are alive!

106 | I CAN'T BELIEVE IT!

The captain warns,
"The water!
Keep bailing out the water!"

Uncle and other people in the cabin
rush to the deck, all crying,
despite the captain warning,
"Go back down! The boat will capsize!"

It is no use.
Some raise their arms
and give thanks toward the ship,
"Thank you, thank you.
Buddha bless you!
Duc Me bless you!
Heaven God bless you!
Kwun Yum bless you!"
Some clap.
Some young men show the victory sign.
Many women kneel on the deck,
facing the bright blue sky,
facing the ship,
praying and crying in Vietnamese,
"Thank you, *Duc Me,*
for listening to our prayers

and saving us!"

Uncle is beaming now.
He keeps shaking his head,
"I can't believe it!
Only the Communist Russians
would come to rescue us!"

I say to him proudly,
"I knew it in my heart!
Remember, 'Not every soldier is mean!'"

107 | NO LONGER A PILE OF DEAD FISH

The captain of the commercial Russian ship
sends two rubber rafts
loaded with food and water to us.

We are no longer a pile of dead fish.

After drinking the water and eating the food,
some of us throw up.
People say it is a good sign:
at least we have something to throw up.
I throw up, too.
I don't mind
this time.

Auntie turns her face away
when Uncle gives her water and food.
Nam offers it to her instead.
She drinks the water
and eats a few crackers.

We feel like a big rock is being lifted from us
after Auntie eats and drinks,
even though she is still acting
like she doesn't want
anything to do with Uncle.

The Russian ship tows our boat
alongside their big ship.
Their captain asks us
if we want to go to Russia.

Some young men say,
"We don't care where we go,
as long as there is a country
that will take us."
They board the Russian ship.

Uncle and the others just thank the captain
for his kindness.
They conclude:
"We have risked our lives
to get out of a communist country.
It doesn't make sense to go back
to another communist country."
They request the kind captain
to just put them on solid ground somewhere,
but not Malaysia.

The captain contacts
Hong Kong by radio.
They decline.

Japan declines.

Singapore declines.

Only Indonesia agrees to take us.

Hooray!

109 | GOODBYE, KINDHEARTED RUSSIAN CAPTAIN

The Russian ship
stays two whole days with us.
They begin to tow our boat
toward Indonesia by daylight.
They repair our boat at night,
for it is not safe to tow
during the high, strong winds.
The winds heave our boat
onto the peaks of the waves,
then plunge it down into the troughs
as we all scream.

After our boat is fixed,
the kindhearted captain keeps towing us.
Now it is just a two-hour journey
to reach our destination.
He draws a map for our captain,
and he gives him instructions
on how to get there.
Before the ship cruises away,
the kindhearted captain gives us
more food
and more water.

People wave at the ship with tears
and thank them
in Vietnamese and Chinese:
"Thank you! You are our saviors!"

"Thank you, captain!
You are a noble man.
I hope you have a good life!"

I do not say anything;
I just wave at them.
I have made up my mind that
someday
I will tell the world
that an unnamed Russian captain
and his crew saved us
on June 17, 1979,
in the South China Sea.
They ended our seven days
of drifting in the sea
and spent two more days with us
repairing our boat.

PART FOUR

June 19, 1979
Indonesia

For a long time,
as the Russian ship sails farther away
and then disappears,
people are still talking
about how lucky we are
to be saved
by the kindhearted captain and his crew.

Then, suddenly, there are
three
loud
gunshots.

We are alert
as the captain stops navigating.
Pirates?
Until
an Indonesian patrol boat
pulls alongside to
question us.
We are already in Indonesian waters.

They let our boat in,
thanks to the kindhearted Russian captain.
We make our way to the closest island,

a remote island,

until our boat hits the sand.

"At last!"

We all are relieved.

Again,

we sleep on the sand.

We still have the rocking sensation,

like before.

But

we are

safe.

111 | SEPARATING?

The next day,
the Red Cross comes
and distributes food to everybody—
the same kind of food that we got before,
when we were in Malaysia.

Some translators help us
fill out forms in English.
We each state our name,
age,
gender,
and nationality,
as well as the names of
any siblings and parents that accompanied us.

Dee Dee and I are considered orphans.
I feel a little uneasy.
Does it mean that
Uncle, Auntie, Nam, and *Dee Dee* and I,
will be separated?

I choose what Uncle chooses:
America is our first choice to go to,
and Canada is the second.

I am glad that
on the third day
we all, including Uncle's family,
are transferred to a temporary camp,
which has five thousand refugees.
We are thrilled.
We are close to being transferred
to a regular camp,
close to being interviewed,
and close to finding a new country
and settling down.

112 | THE HOUSING

The housing for the camp on Coconut Island
(that's what we call it because of the coconut trees)
is row after row of long, simple sheds.
The roofs are made of logs
covered with palm fronds
over plastic sheets
to keep the rain out.
They are all supported by poles.

There are no walls.

Inside, the long shed
is divided into many small rooms
by three-foot-tall barriers of twigs.
There is no privacy.
We can look through the entire long shed.
But we have no complaints.

Uncle pays two taels of gold
to obtain a room.
Others, like the single young men,
who don't want to pay or don't have gold,
sleep on the ground outside,
facing the sky.

I am very thankful that
Uncle hasn't excluded us
from staying in their room.

We make our own beds
by using poles and boards nailed together
about four or five inches
above the ground,
to avoid the insects.

But Auntie refuses to share a bed with Uncle.
I share a bed with her
while the others all share another one together.
We get "new" clothes from the bags of clothing
in the office shed.
They have been donated
by different countries.
Everyone just picks out clothes
that fit them.

I am very glad that
I finally have another pair of sandals
to wear.
The top of the sandals that Dao gave me
have torn.

But I do not throw them away.

I treasure them

to help me remember

Dao.

113 | MY REWARD

Auntie is staying inside all the time.
I help make a stove
by digging a hole
and placing a few rocks around it
like Auntie did in Malaysia.
Starting the fire
is quite a frustrating challenge.
I don't mind
the smoke that stings my eyes.
I don't mind
the charcoal
that soils my face and arms
and the heat from the fire
that makes me perspire
like rain.

I only consider that
cooking the meal
and brewing the tea and coffee
are the best ways to show my appreciation
to Uncle and Auntie.

And I am so pleased that
Auntie is willing
to eat a couple of spoonfuls of rice

and sip some coffee,
as my big reward.

Uncle is very pleased.
He quietly says to me,
"Thank you, Lam.
I hope she will gain her strength back."

I reply confidently,
"She will. Give her some time."

114 | THE LAST THING I WANT TO DO

The pit toilets are big holes in the ground
away from the sheds,
the same as the ones in Malaysia.
They are enclosed with palm leaves,
instead of using grass mats,
and supported by poles.

But some people don't bother
to use the pit toilets.
They just let children urinate
or defecate on the ground
and don't obey the rule of filling the old ones
and digging new ones
if they get caught.
So going there is the last thing
I want to do,
except to accompany Auntie,
who is barely able to walk.

And I miss Dao.

115 | WHERE ARE MY FRIENDS?

Uncle will not allow us
to go into the woods
to gather firewood.
Only he and other adults go.

I look back to the day
of the tragedy.
I can't help but regret it once again.
If that day we hadn't gone for firewood,
if that day Dao hadn't kept her eyes
on the twins
instead of paying attention
to where she was stepping,
then she might have lived.

And I think of Twin Number One.
If I had a chance to see him again,
should I tell him
Dao's secret?

Should I?

I think about Jan and Ming.
Where are they?
Are they drifting in the ocean like we did,

or

are they as safe as I am now?

I miss the kind herbal doctor
who treated *Dee Dee* for free.
I have always wondered
if Dao would have still been alive
if he had been around
when the snake struck.

Will I see him again?

So where are they?
Are they all okay?
I feel
we are just like the floating clouds.
Perhaps,
someday,
we might drift
into one another
again.
Who knows?

I hope they are
safe and well.

116 | DRINKING WATER

There is no well around;
only a stream
that flows down from a nearby hill.
Some people just wash their clothing
or take their bath in the stream
near the campsite.
So all the water near the camp
is contaminated.

To get clean drinking water
is a hard task.
We have to compete
with the strong male teens
who obtain water for others for a little cash.
Dee Dee, Nam, and I have to climb
higher
and
higher
up the hill
each day
to fetch water from the stream,
despite the risk of falling.

117 | AN EPIDEMIC BREAKS OUT

An epidemic breaks out.
Many small children
and old people die each day
and are buried at the foot of the hill.

In our shed,
Auntie gets sick first.
I get diarrhea and vomit.
Sometimes I feel like I am on fire.
Other times, I shiver all over, feeling cold.
I can't cook and
I can't take care of Auntie.
Uncle takes over my chores.

I fear I am going to die.
I tell myself, *I can't die.*
I have to take care of *Dee Dee;*
I have to take care of Auntie, Uncle, and Nam;
I have to be reunited with *Baba;*
I have to see Snow White for Dao.

There are Vietnamese doctors
on the big Red Cross ship
that anchors off the beach
who provide me

with medicine.

I survive.

But not Auntie.
She doesn't even fight.

118 | MOURNING AUNTIE

Uncle doesn't think it's wise for us
to see Auntie be buried.
He fears we could get sick
since the burial site is so
contaminated.

For some reason,
losing Auntie
does not devastate me as much as
when Dao suddenly passed away.

But I am worried about Nam.
I hardly see him shed tears
the whole time.
I wish he would cry and just let out
the pain of losing his *ma*.

Uncle is distraught.
He stays inside the shed and hardly speaks.
But he smokes excessively
and leaves cigarette butts scattered
all over the ground,
until one day,
he starts hitting his head
on the pole of the shed

in desperation.
"It's all my fault.
If I hadn't urged them to leave . . .
If I hadn't gone fishing . . .
It's all my fault. . . ."

Nam, *Dee Dee*, and I
all throw ourselves on him,
crying, begging, and pulling him away
from the pole.
"Don't do it, *Cha*. . . ."
"Please don't, Uncle. . . ."
"Please don't hurt yourself, Uncle. . . ."
We all embrace him
weeping,
mourning,
while the small children outside
watch.

119 | CONCERN

I am very concerned about Uncle.
His hair seems to be turning gray
suddenly,
after he has lost his daughter and wife
in such a short period of time.

He still stays in the shed with Nam
most of the time,
except when he goes out to gather firewood.
Maybe it is their way of mourning.
I don't know.
I hope he doesn't turn out like Auntie.
The image of her shrunken, lifeless body
is always in my mind,
and I can't easily chase it away.

If there were some way to help him
ease his guilt and grief,
I wouldn't mind
going to get the firewood,
fetching the water, and
doing all the other chores,
as his daughter would.

120 | MAKING NEW FRIENDS

I often keep an eye on Uncle and Nam
to make sure they eat enough and drink water.
I really fear that
they will turn out like Auntie.

I feel so helpless,
with no one whom
I can trust to express
my fears.

I meet sisters, Lai and Wai,
while washing clothes.
Just as we did,
they left Vietnam by boat but arrived
a few months ahead of us.

They tell me
some people have been seeing ghosts,
especially the lady ghost in white
who has no legs,
but floats around the pit toilets,
which are close to where
the dead people are being buried.

They say the ghosts can't rest in peace.

They didn't reach their destination,
but died halfway.

I fear that Dao has already turned into a ghost,
wandering around to find her family,
or to see her secret lover.
I fear that Auntie has already turned into a ghost,
a brokenhearted ghost,
wandering around to find Dao.

I feel chills
as I try to shake away the images.

I am so glad when
Lai and Wai ask me to go to the latrine with them,
to avoid being hassled by the rude men
and to be brave together if we encounter
any ghosts.

I am so glad when
Lai and Wai ask me to fetch water with them
at the upper stream.
They don't tell me their secrets like Dao did,
and I don't tell them mine.

Still, I enjoy being with them.
I have someone to do things with,
and I have someone my age to talk to,
to ease the fears
inside me.

Dee Dee makes friends with their brother, Ding.

They like to watch other people sell goods.
There are boat captains who can speak English
and will take a ferry
to a nearby island to buy goods,
then sell them to the other refugees.

I tell Uncle about it.
I wish he would go to the island
to get out,
to ease the guilt and grief of
losing a daughter and wife.

But he shows no interest in going.

121 | WAITING TO BE INTERVIEWED

We got the wrong information
when we were in the camp in Malaysia—
that people would be interviewed
only after they had been placed
in a regular camp.

It is here in this temporary camp
where we will unexpectedly
be interviewed.
Everybody waits for their name
to be called
over the loudspeaker.

There are several small sheds,
built at the beach near the Red Cross Ship.
Delegates from many countries, such as
Germany,
America,
Israel,
Australia,
France, and
England
come
at various times.

Each time, as the loudspeaker blares,
everybody drops what they are doing
to listen.
They will smile
like a morning sunshine glow
if their name is called.

The ones who haven't been called
do not lose hope.
For they know
someday
they will get out of this refugee camp
and start a new life
somewhere.

It is just a matter of time.
They are patient.
They are optimistic.

One day,
my name and *Dee Dee*'s
are called for an interview.
Our important moment has arrived.
I am thrilled,
yet also filled with some sadness.
They did not call Uncle's name
or Nam's name.
Will it mean that
we will be separated for real
this time?

But when he hears our names being called,
Uncle breaks into a big smile—
the first one we've seen since Auntie passed.
He congratulates us
while I still feel a little guilty.

He reminds us not to be late
for this important moment.
He instructs us
to be there half an hour earlier
than the appointment time.
"Otherwise," he concludes,
"they may put your name

at the bottom,
and you will have to wait
all over again."

So we do what he tells us.

Through the translator,
I tell the delegate that
my *baba* is in San Francisco,
and he is working in a Chinese restaurant.
I can't provide the address,
which was written
on the underside of *Dee Dee*'s shirt
and now can't be read anymore
because it has faded.

It delays our processing.
I do not feel discontent,
because the delegate says
he will try to locate my *baba*.

Some people
whose names haven't been called
gather outside the delegate sheds
to collect information from the ones
who have just come out
from being interviewed.
They want to know
how to prepare for the questions
when their time comes.

I tell Uncle I failed to provide *Baba*'s address.
Uncle comforts us by saying,
"I think your case will be processed very soon
because you are considered orphans.
Orphans will have priority."

I hope what he says
is right.
I hope what he says
is wrong.

Very often, before falling asleep,
I have quietly asked *Kwun Yum*
to bless Uncle and Nam
so their names will be called.

Kwun Yum hears me.
Three weeks later,
Uncle and Nam are interviewed.
They don't have any relatives in either
America or Canada.
They have to wait
longer
to find someone
who will sponsor them.

I am wishing that
Baba could sponsor them.
I don't want to leave Uncle and Nam
behind.

To my surprise,
in the days after he's had his interview,
Uncle goes out from the shed
once in a while
to gather information on

how they can be sponsored
by the people from America
or Canada.

125 | ON OUR OWN

After a total of six months
of living in the temporary camp,
Dee Dee and I and a group of other people
are transferred
to a regular camp.
Again, Uncle and Nam are excluded.
There are rumors
that people who are transferred
to the regular camp
are close to finding a country.

I have felt so safe,
so secure,
while we have been with Uncle's family,
who are like a part of me.
But now,
we will be on our own.

I am not scared.
I know how to make a bed.
I know how to make a stove with stones.
I know how to fetch water.
I know how to get firewood.
I know how to cook the food,
and I will ask *Dee Dee* to accompany me

to the toilet.
I know we will be okay.

But I'm not sure about Uncle,
whose life has been
in a downward spiral.
And now we are leaving them
behind.

Uncle thinks that we are afraid
to be on our own.
He comforts me, saying gently,
"Don't be afraid.
The staff of the Red Cross
are good people with kind hearts.
Let them know
if you have any problems."

"But . . . who is going to cook for you
and wash your clothes?"
I am embarrassed
to tell him the fear I have
about him.

Uncle lets out a laugh.
He says,
"While you've been here,
we've depended on you.
Now Nam and I
will depend on
ourselves.
So don't worry."

He gives us their only pot,

two bowls, two pairs of chopsticks,
a few candles with matches,
a few packages of mosquito repellent,
and some Indonesian money.
"Just in case," he says.
I refuse his cash.
He insists:
"Having a little money in hand
will help."

I turn my head
and do not want him to see
my eyes.

He instructs *Dee Dee,*
"Listen to your sister.
Don't do anything stupid
like you did when you jumped off the boat.
And always accompany your sister
whenever she goes to the toilet."

Dee Dee and Nam
don't want to be separated.
They exchange the shells
they have been collecting.

I want to say goodbye to Auntie.
I want to thank her for her kindness
in blending us into their family.
I want to tell her
I will never forget her and Dao.

Uncle doesn't think
we should go to pay our respects
to Auntie.
He's afraid
that I will get sick once again.
He thanks me for my sincere thoughts
instead.

Dee Dee and I are about
to board the bus,
while Lai, Wai, and many other people
stand next to the bus and
wish us luck.

Before we get in,
Uncle, as if unwilling to part from us,
instructs us once more:
"Be careful.
There are many good people,
but there are many bad people, too.
You must use your own judgment."

I nod
as I try hard to keep my emotions in check
and prepare to board the bus.
But at the last moment,
Dee Dee and I both
run back
to embrace Uncle.

Uncle tousles our hair and
says,
"We will meet again.

We will meet again."

The bus honks,
rushing us to board.

So
we part.

I wave at him and Nam with my face
washed by tears.
I want to tell him to take care.
I want to tell him
he is our noble man.
I want to tell him
we will see him again.

But I can't make my words come out.

I just cry as the bus turns
and leaves them behind.
I cry the whole time,
even after we get off the bus.

Mr. and Mrs. Pham,
who were on the same boat as us,

say to me,
"Are you related to Mr. Nguyen?
He asked us to keep an eye on you both.
We promised him."

That makes me shed more tears as I say,
"I don't know how to repay him. . . ."

Some say
it is the biggest refugee camp
in Indonesia.
They say
there are tens of thousands of people there.
For me,
without Uncle and Nam,
there is nobody!

129 | THE NEW CAMP

There are rows and rows of big houses
that have been built with real wooden boards.
Each house is divided by
four long wooden beds.
Each bed can sleep twenty-five people.
People place plastic sheets
between them for privacy.

There are mint,
bitter melon,
and green vegetables
that are popular in our hometown
growing around the houses,
planted by the early comers
who are still waiting.

I have missed those vegetables.
I miss home.

There is continuously running water
from a refugee-constructed bamboo sluice
flowing from the creek
that eventually empties into a
small, man-made reservoir.
Now, I don't need to climb up and down

between the thorny bushes
to get water.

There are kerosene and clay stoves
in a big public kitchen,
which only has a roof,
that people can take turns using.
Some people who can afford it
use their own kerosene stoves
because getting firewood is not easy.
Many people who cut firewood
for their own use
or sell it to the other refugees
are often lost in the remote jungle
and never return.
I am so thankful
that Uncle gave me the cash "just in case."

I like the toilet the most.
It is built of wood, a solid house.
And it has water to wash away the waste,
even though it is still stinky.

There are doctors
and a place to mail letters

and receive letters.
I had never thought of using Uncle's money
to send a letter to Uncle or to home
because I had never sent
or received
a letter before.
There is a place to exchange money
and a big TV screen outdoors.
But no free English lessons.

I miss the English lessons
Uncle gave us.

Mr. and Mrs. Pham
do what they have promised Uncle.
They let us squeeze
into the same unit with them.
They let me use their kerosene stove
that they purchased
from a small shop run by refugees
to cook for *Dee Dee* and me.
I want to pay them for the kerosene,
but they say Uncle gave them some cash
in case we needed it.
I almost shed tears in front of them.

We do not eat together with them.

When *Dee Dee* and I eat outside the house,
I often wonder:
Are Uncle and Nam having their meal, too?
Are they still staying inside the shed
like Auntie did?

I am very frustrated.
How I wish I could talk to them.
How I wish I could see them.

131 | LIKE A VILLAGE

The campsite isn't
as dark as the other camp was.
Many people have kerosene lanterns
or flashlights.

There are
coffee houses,
noodle shops,
and other small stores
that sell simple daily necessities,
operated by refugees
who have been here longer in this camp.

Dee Dee and I hunger
for a bowl of pho to share
with the money Uncle gave us.
I finally squash my desire,
thinking about what Uncle said—
that the money was for "just in case."

So *Dee Dee* watches
other people devour the noodles,
with his saliva
almost dripping down his chin.

Many people have small portable radios.
They get the Chinese channel from Australia
so they aren't isolated
from the outside world.

If someone puts his radio on top of the counter
when I cook or wash dishes,
I often perk up my ears
so I can listen in, too.

We are most appreciative of the
big movie screen outdoors
that is the highlight of our life in the camp.

In the evenings,
sometimes they play Taiwanese movies;
sometimes they play Hong Kong movies;
sometimes they play Vietnamese movies.
Despite the fact that there are no seats available,
and we have to stand up to watch the movies,
we don't complain,
for this helps satisfy our thirst
for reminders of home.

Once, they even show us the

Olympic Games from 1976.
The screen doesn't have any translation,
only English language.
It doesn't matter.
We just watch the action
and let out a cry of disappointment
when an athlete loses
or cheer
when an athlete wins.

132 | UNITED WITH MY COUSIN

One evening,
after we have been living in the new camp
for about two months,
we run into Cousin Tam at the movies!

She has a hard time believing
we are still alive.

They thought that our boat had capsized
and we were all dead.

I tell Cousin Tam all about what happened to us,
especially about Uncle's family.

She embraces both of us and says
she is going to take care of us.

Cousin Tam and her family left Vietnam
two months after we did
and were transferred to this camp three months ago.

She says my *ma*
almost had a nervous breakdown
after they assumed our boat had capsized.

It dawns on me that
I never thought of what my family's reaction
would be
when they hadn't heard from us.

I just didn't think of it.
I only told them
once in a while, silently,
that we were safe.

So I immediately write a letter home.
Cousin Tam helps me mail the letter.

"Your *daigo* is okay," she tells me.
"He was captured and put in jail,
but before I left home he was freed
when your *ma* bailed him out."

That is what I have suspected for a long time.
I have never had a bad dream about him.

I wish I had a way to inform Uncle that
I finally have some of my family with me.
He will not be worried about us
if he hears this news.

133 | LIVING WITH COUSIN TAM

Cousin Tam, who is in her thirties,
thanks the Phams for keeping an eye on us.
And the Phams are happy that
we finally have our own relatives
to care for us.

We move into Cousin Tam's living space.
The space isn't as roomy as the Phams'.
We squeeze together when we sleep.
Cousin Tam's family does not complain,
and neither do we.

Cousin Tam has planted a variety of vegetables
around their house.
She cooks a big bowl of fresh lettuce
and yard long beans
just for *Dee Dee* and me.
We devour the vegetables with
nothing else.
They are the first fresh vegetables we have eaten
since we left home.

I wish I could share them with
Uncle and Nam.

Life in this big camp
is somewhat easier.
We don't need to collect firewood.
Cousin Tam also uses a kerosene stove.
We don't need to fetch water.
We have a lot of spare time to just do
nothing.

I get tired of watching someone
sell his goods.
I am bored of just strolling on the beach
with my cousin's two girls,
who are six and eight.
And I still have a bad feeling
about the open sea.

The only things I do are help Cousin Tam cook,
wash clothes,
and tend the vegetable plants.

My mind is often occupied with thoughts
of Uncle and Nam.
My concerns can't be eased.
At night,
not knowing what is happening with them

tortures me even more,
like half of me is melting away.
I can't easily fall asleep.
All I can do is keep praying
that Uncle will not isolate himself
in their shed like Auntie did.

Dee Dee is restless, too.
Several times
he has gotten into fights with other kids
and ended up with a bloody nose.
Cousin Tam has restricted him
to staying in the house.
It drives him crazy.
He says he wants to run away.

Cousin Tam asks,
"Where are you going to run away to?
There is water on all sides!"

Dee Dee misses Nam
badly.

135 | ON MY BIRTHDAY

As before,
I just live day to day,
without knowing the day of the week
or the date of the month,
until Cousin Tam
suddenly gives me *lai see* money,
saying that today is March 7
and that I have turned twelve.

Nothing is special on my birthday.
It is just another day—full of unknowns.
Then I see *Dee Dee*,
who is playing around Cousin's house,
suddenly run to someone
and embrace him.

I am puzzled
until *Dee Dee* lets out a cry.

It is Uncle!
He smiles at me and says,
"I finally found you!
Didn't I say we would meet again?"

He and Nam were transferred to this big camp

about a month ago.
They have been trying to find out
if we were also located in this camp,
but they didn't have a way of doing it,
until one day he read my name
on the announcement board,
saying I had a letter.
He was sure we were in the same camp.
He put more effort than ever
into looking for us.
Since there are so many people,
the officials just use the person's name and
the numbers of the boat they were in
to distinguish each group.

I am glad Uncle saw my name.
I don't even know the number of our boat.

So this is not just another day!
Nothing is more precious
than this reunion with Uncle and Nam—
my best birthday present ever!

136 | LETTER FROM *BABA*

The letter is from *Baba* in San Francisco.
He, too, is stunned to discover
we are still alive.
He says
he is trying his best
to get us to America.

In the letter is a check
for two hundred US dollars.
Uncle helps me exchange it
into Indonesian money.
I return the money Uncle gave me
for "just in case."

To celebrate our reunion with Uncle and Nam,
the next day, I use *Baba*'s money
to invite them, Mr. and Mrs. Pham,
and Cousin Tam's whole family
to eat pho, which we haven't had for ages,
at a small, one-table-only noodle shop.

Uncle is very happy for us.
He says we will probably go to America
to be with *Baba* soon.
He says he'd hate to see *Dee Dee* and me be

unable to speak English
when we first get there,
so he will continue our English lessons.

This promise causes my eyes
to cloud with tears.
I thought he would
never resume teaching us again
because of the pain he has carried.
I don't know what to say,
but stammer in a shaking voice, "Thank you."

And it is the first night
I can easily fall asleep
since we parted from Uncle
three months ago.

137 | MY APPRECIATION

I don't want Uncle to spend more of his gold
for us.
I voluntarily buy
five exercise books,
five pens,
chalks,
and a small piece of board as a blackboard
from the store in the camp.

Without Uncle's knowledge,
I surprise him by
presenting him
with an English/Vietnamese dictionary
that I had a boat captain buy for me
to express
our appreciation.

He says it is exactly what he needs
and he will treasure it
forever.

Uncle now has three old students plus
two of Cousin's children.

As before,
we have class in the morning
in an area not far from our living space.
He teaches us the ABC letters
and some simple words.
It is much easier to understand now
than when he taught us in the past
because he can write the words down
clearly on the board
and we can actually write them
in our exercise books.

But sometimes
the lessons dredge up memories
of when Dao and Auntie
were with us.

I try to shake my head
to get rid of these images.
I try to tell myself that
no matter what I do,
no matter where I go,

Dao and Auntie can never
come back.

I guess Uncle
also has these sad moments, too,
as I notice that sometimes
he is very quiet.
It makes me want to hold his hands.

I hope someday,
despite the grief of his loss,
he will find the strength
to heal,
to move on.

I hope.

139 | UNCLE'S STUDENTS

In no time
Uncle's students grow from five to ten.
The newcomers are *Dee Dee*'s friends
who have fought with *Dee Dee* before.

Unlike the other tutors,
Uncle doesn't charge a fee.
He humbly says his knowledge of English
isn't very advanced.
All he asks from the new students is that
they provide their own pens and books.

After their parents find out
that he doesn't have a wife with him,
they take turns cooking for him and Nam,
to show their appreciation,
while Cousin provides them with fresh vegetables.

140 | UNCLE HEALS HIMSELF BY HELPING OTHERS

Uncle is very busy.
He doesn't have time to smoke.

When he's not teaching,
I often see him looking up things in the dictionary
while sitting on a rock in front of his living space.
He says he needs to improve his own English,
as well.

He makes friends with the parents
who volunteer to bring him food,
as well as Cousin and her husband.
Uncle is no longer
staying inside his living space
as he did
right after Auntie passed away.

I guess his wounds are
healing
gradually
from him helping others.

Seeing his father moving out of
his darkest stage,

Nam laughs together with *Dee Dee*
and the other boys in the class.

Nothing is more of a treasure than
seeing Uncle as he was
before the tragedies.

The staff processes our case very quickly.
Not long after reading *Baba*'s letter,
Dee Dee and I have a physical exam.
After we have lived in the regular camp
for almost half a year,
we are told that
we will go to America.

The day before we are to leave,
I prepare a special meal
of pho,
just for Uncle and Nam.
We eat at their living space,
just the four of us,
like before.

But we are not that hungry.

Uncle says to me,
"Now the needle inside my heart
has finally been removed.
You both have endured such hardships
because I brought you with us.
Now I am very happy
you are joining your *baba*

and will have a good life."

I assure him that
we are so lucky that
we have had them on this journey.
I assure him that
they have not just been a noble man and woman;
they have been just like parents to us.

So I give an eye signal to *Dee Dee*.
Like *Baba* did to his ma
before he left home,
Dee Dee and I bow three times,
solemnly and respectfully,
to Uncle,
as if he were
our *baba*.

I can't sleep,
again.
I have so many, many things to tell Dao.

I tell her that I can't fulfill my duty
of taking care of Uncle and Nam and her *ma*.
I tell her that sometimes
people can't control their own fate.

I tell her that Uncle and Nam have to stay here
longer.
I am not worried about them now
as much as I was
when I first parted from them.

I tell her that
she doesn't need to worry about them, either.
Uncle has finally come out of his depression.
By helping others,
he has healed himself.

I tell her that now Uncle has many friends
and is respected by many parents,
so I am no longer feeling so sad
about leaving them behind.

I tell her that someday
we all will meet again.
Then we will all go to Disneyland
to see Snow White
and to the mountains to see snow
for her.

I know Dao is listening,
even though she doesn't say a word.

The International Refugee Organization (IRO)
lets us borrow the money for airline tickets
without charging us interest.
The cost is $325 for one person,
half of what the adults pay.

On June 7, 1980,
I leave everything behind,
except the two pairs of chopsticks
Uncle gave us,
Dao's sandals,
our exercise books,
and the gratitude for Uncle.

Dee Dee takes only the shells
he and Nam exchanged.

We and the other refugees
are given a white travel bag
as we get ready to board a boat at the ferry.
We will transfer to a big ship
that will sail to Singapore.
We will spend two days in Singapore.
Then we will fly to San Francisco.

Before we board the boat,
many people say, "Have a good life!"
They hope that the next boat
will be for them.
I say goodbye to my cousin and her family,
to the Phams,
and to my friends.
I wait until the last moment
to say goodbye to Uncle and Nam,
for my throat
is already feeling
like something is choking me.

So I try very hard to avoid looking into
Uncle's eyes,
for fear I can't control myself.
It is *Dee Dee*
who wails
as Uncle and Nam embrace him.

Suddenly, all my tears,
which I have been trying hard
to keep stored away,
drain out
like a waterfall.

I can't help it.
I hug them, too.
I say, "I will never forget you, Uncle."

Uncle wipes his eyes, too.
He pats me and says,
"You have a good life.
You study hard.
We will meet again.
Okay?"

Cousin parts us from Uncle and Nam.
She urges us to board the boat.
I clean my nose and sob,
"You take good care, Uncle.
We will meet again."

I hear someone ask as I
unwillingly head toward the boat,
"Who is that man to this girl?"

I turn and reply,
"He has been a father to me!"

On the way to Singapore,
I am the quietest passenger, and I sit
motionless,
even though the others are amazed
by the big ship.

Two days later,
on the plane to San Francisco,
Dee Dee and the others are fascinated
by the new experience of
taking a plane
and by the floating clouds
that surround us.

He tells me
what he wants to see first,
while I am wondering
if *Baba* will still recognize us.
It is the first time
since I left Vietnam
that I have really thought about *Baba*.

I am wondering
if *Baba* will meet us at the airport.

I am wondering
if I will like America.

I am wondering
if people will pick on us
because we don't speak English.

The plane lands.
Many passengers applaud.
We are safe in this new country.

We, the refugees, follow the translator and
enter the terminal.
We clear customs.
We are fingerprinted by immigration.
Then we follow the translator into a big room
where many people
are waiting.

They are holding signs with names on them.
My heart suddenly beats like an
elephant trumpeting.
I am afraid to look at the crowd.
I am afraid *Baba* might not be there. . . .

Then I hear *Dee Dee* call out,
"Baba! Baba!"

Baba looks just the same as
when he left two years ago.
But he stares at us
like he is seeing ghosts.

Then he rushes toward us and embraces us.
He cries, "Oh, I thought I had lost both of you!"

We bury our faces into his chest
and cry.
We hold each other
for a long time.

In the taxi on the way to where *Baba* lives,
Dee Dee looks outside and tells *Baba*
what he wants to buy and
what he wants to see.

I just hold *Baba*'s hand
the whole time.
At this moment,
I do not look out of the window
at the high buildings
and the cars snaking along curves in the road.
I don't want anything:
not Disneyland,
not real snow.
I just want my *baba*.

He is enough.

EPILOGUE

In June of 1980, thirteen months after we left our home in Vietnam, *Dee Dee* and I were finally reunited with our *baba* in America.

We enrolled in school right away. We studied English all day long with other refugees. We all started with the ABCs, which I already knew because of Uncle.

Baba paid back the cost of our airplane tickets to the International Refugee Organization.

Life in America was good, but it was much different from Vietnam. In school I was teased a lot by the students—the white, black, and even ABC's—American-born Chinese. So was *Dee Dee*. They laughed at our pronunciation of English words. Sometimes they even told us to go back to where we came from. It didn't bother me as much as it did *Dee Dee*. Compared to what we had gone through, this teasing and laughing were nothing! I could face anything!

My *daigo* later escaped again and then came to the United States. Today he lives in Australia with his family.

After I graduated from high school, I got married. Together with my husband, we opened a Chinese restaurant in South Carolina and raised three kids. *Dee Dee* also worked in our restaurant. But he wasn't as lucky as me. His wife died from diabetes and left him with no children. He still remains single.

We applied for my *ma* to come to the states in 1985, and she was able to come in 1990. We united happily in an emotional reunion after eleven years of separation. Unfortunately, my *ah mah* didn't make it. She died before my *ma* came here.

After my cousin and her family left Indonesia not long after we did, they settled down in Canada.

Now I have fulfilled my desire to tell the world about our journey and the kindhearted Russian captain. I don't know if he is still alive. But I hope that he and his descendants have had a good life. He will live in my heart forever. And I also thank the Indonesian government for accepting us to stay in their country until we could leave for America.

—Lam Chan, June 2013

GLOSSARY

• *ah mah*—[ah mah] term for one's "paternal grandmother" in Cantonese, which is the most common Chinese dialect of ethnic Chinese living in Vietnam

• auntie—a respectful term to address a lady, not necessarily related

• *baba*—[bah-bah] "father" in Cantonese

• *bà ngoại*—[bah wai] "maternal grandmother" in Vietnamese

• bow—[bough] the front of a ship or boat that sticks out when it is underway

• *cha*—[jah] "father" in Vietnamese

• China and Vietnam War—also called the Sino-Vietnamese War or the Third Indochina War, this short-lived war was initiated by Deng Xiaoping, the leader of China during this time, in support of their ally the Khmer Rouge of Cambodia, because of the mistreatment of ethnic Chinese minority in Vietnam and the occupation of the Spratly Islands, which were claimed by China. This brief war between the border of Vietnam and China officially lasted from February 17, 1979 to March 16, 1979. Tens of thousands of lives were lost on both sides of the conflict. Yet the war did not receive much attention in the West.

• Cholon, Vietnam—Chinatown in Saigon

• *daigo*—[die goh] a respectful term for "older brother" in Cantonese

• *dee dee*—[dee dee] the commonly used Cantonese term for younger brother

• dragon bone—a slang term for the keel of a ship, the bottom-most structural part of the ship that runs from the bow to the stern

• *Duc Me*—[duke mayah] the Virgin Mary in Vietnamese

• *giúp tôi!*—[zep doi] "Help me!" in Vietnamese

• hatch—an opening on the deck of a ship through which there is access to parts of the ship below the deck

• Heaven God—Chinese name for the universal God

• IRO—International Refugee Organization

• *Kwun Yum*—[kwoon yum] the "Goddess of Mercy" in Cantonese, also called *Guānyīn* in Mandarin. She is the most important Chinese deity.

• *lai see*—[lie see] "lucky money" in Cantonese. It is money given in red envelopes to children or younger relatives by adults, especially at Chinese New Year or for birthdays.

• *ma*—[mah] "mother" in Cantonese

• My Tho—a city settled by Chinese fleeing China in the 1680s and now considered the gateway to the Mekong Delta

• *pau pau*—[paw paw] term for one's "maternal grandmother" in Cantonese

• pho—[fuh] Vietnamese rice noodle soup, served with meat, herbs, and bean sprouts

• sampan—[sam pan] a relatively flat-bottomed Chinese wooden boat, generally used for transportation and often used as a traditional fishing boat

• tael—[teel] a unit of measure weighing about one and one-third ounce

• uncle—a respectful term to address an elder man who may or may not be a relative

ACKNOWLEDGMENTS

Thank you so much to my friends Chou and Yeung for sharing with me details of their gripping journey to freedom in 1979.

My heartfelt gratitude goes to the unnamed refugees I talked with in 1992 at the Hong Kong refugee camp, who provided me more details of their escapes and gave me the inspiration to develop the story of Uncle and his family.

My sincere appreciation to my agent, Adria Goetz of Martin Literary Management, for believing in my work; to my publisher, Sonali Fry of Yellow Jacket, for liking this work and patiently editing it repeatedly; to my copy editors, Dave Barrett and Christina Solazzo, who checked this manuscript thoroughly; and to Wendy Cheng, my friend who provided my name in Chinese characters.

Last, but not least, thanks to my husband, Phillip Russell, who is my first editor and who has helped me in many ways in my adopted country.